Ann Pilling was born and b̶... some of her early years were spent in North Wales very like the one in the story. 'And there really *was* a sealed room,' she says.

She is married with two sons, and now lives in Oxford with her family and two cats. She has written a number of books for children, including *Henry's Leg*, which won the 1986 Guardian Award, and four ghost stories.

On the Lion's Side was nominated for the 1989 Carnegie Medal.

Ann Pilling

ON THE LION'S SIDE

PIPER BOOKS
in association with William Heinemann Ltd

Verses from 'The Cry of Elishá after Elija'
from *Song at the Year's Turning* © 1955
by R. S. Thomas, published by Grafton Books,
are used by kind permission of the author.

First published by William Heinemann Ltd
This Piper edition published 1990 by Pan Books Ltd,
Cavaye Place, London, SW10 9PG
in association with William Heinemann Ltd.
10 9 8 7 6 5 4 3

ISBN 0 330 31046 1

Printed in England by Clays Ltd, St Ives plc

for Irene

'Forsan et haec olim meminisse iuvabit'

'The chariot of Israel came,
And the bold, beautiful knights,
To free from his close prison
The friend who was my delight;
Cold is my cry over the vast deep shaken,
Bereft was I, for he was taken.

I yield, since no wisdom lies
In seeking to go his way;
A man without knowledge am I
Of the quality of his joy;
Yet living souls, a prodigious number,
Bright-faced as dawn, invest God's chamber.

The friends that we loved well,
Though they vanished far from our sight,
In a new country were found
Beyond this vale of night;
O blest are they, without pain or fretting
In the sun's light that knows no setting.'

The Cry of Elisha after Elija
R.S. Thomas (from the Welsh of Thomas Williams,
Bethesda'r Fro)

CHAPTER ONE

'I could kill him,' Robert shouted, staring at the wreckage, 'I could bloody well kill him.'

'Stop shouting,' his sister said 'and don't swear, it's wicked.'

Rebecca, known to the family as Ping, was ten and a half and going through a religious phase with her best friend Sally. Robert was thirteen, bony and big with size eleven feet, a large nose and a thatch of coarse blond hair. Red-haired Ping was quite pretty but Nick was the really beautiful one, Nick the five-year-old monster who'd wrecked this bedroom with his little friend Craig, while Robert was at school. He might look like an angel but at this precise moment his big ugly brother felt like smashing his face in.

'I'm going down,' Ping said. 'I'm not staying here to be yelled at.'

'I'm *not* yelling. I'm just – well, how would you like it?'

Ping shrugged. 'I wouldn't, but there's a ridiculous lot of clutter up here.'

'It's tidy clutter,' Robert said fiercely, 'it's quite organised. And that's not the point. He had no right –'

'Why don't you tell Mum and Dad about it?' Ping interrupted, 'instead of just moaning to me. Anyhow,' she added mysteriously, 'in this life nobody has "rights". I have no rights, you have no rights, they have no rights,' and she glided through the door like a nun.

Robert felt his limited patience giving out. It was a bit much when your ten-year-old sister started lecturing you about 'life'.

'What's the point in telling Mum?' he called after her. 'She won't *do* anything. She never does.'

'Don't shout.'

'Oh . . . *knickers*.' And he slammed the door.

He kicked through the debris on the carpet, went across to the window and looked out, staring blindly at the familiar scene while he tried to get a grip on himself. Three floors below the rush hour traffic was already building up, and in about ten minutes there'd be solid queues all along Chester Avenue.

You could climb through this window and get out on to the tiny balcony outside quite easily. Nick and Craig could have done that. It'd be just like Nick to go right to the edge, peep over and fall off. He'd have to put a lock on it. Why couldn't *Dad* see to things like this, though? Why were the practical boring things always left to him?

Beyond Chester Avenue there were other roads lined with big trees and the same kind of houses. Then the land was all split up by factories and railway lines with his school somewhere in the middle. Before you got into the town there was a great stripe of dark water. Flying off it sometimes, like fat seagulls, were huge blodges of white foam, detergent waste from a chemical plant on the edge of town. There were three canals, too, and they gave off a great stink when the weather was hot; so did the river Mersey. And that was their town, Buckden Heath.

He shut the window in disgust and decided to nail it up until he could get a lock. Dad would never get round to it.

As he hunted for his tools he was forced to take a proper look at what Nick and Craig had done, and when he found his hammer he felt like using it on them. For a start, they'd obviously been trampolining on his bed. It now lurched down at a 45 degree angle and his bedding was in a great heap on the floor. They'd been into his coin collection too, and his stamps, and all his tapes had been emptied from their boxes. One of them had been pulled right out and lay in coils on the table like a heap of brown spaghetti.

The worst thing was the *Mary Rose*. It was an elaborate construction kit that he'd been working on since Christmas. Hours of his life had gone into that, long peaceful hours when he'd been up here by himself, listening to tapes and thinking. Now it lay in ruins on the carpet.

Robert threw himself on to the collapsing bed and stared at the ceiling, thinking about evil Nick and whether his parents would do anything about him, about holy Ping and human rights. And he thought of himself too, and where he fitted into this crazy family.

He didn't, that's why things like this got him down so much, why he couldn't 'ride' them, to borrow Mum's phrase. Nothing ruffled her; she 'rode' everything.

'You're a funniosity,' she'd remarked the other week. He probably was, too, a bit of a loner with his collections and his Airfix models and his classical tapes. He was just 'old-fashioned' compared with the rest of the family, that's what she'd really meant.

Ping hadn't been too bad till she'd palled up with Sally from down the road, but Robert had gone off her recently. This religious craze had started when they'd joined Sally's church youth club and she'd gone right over the top with it; she was always ticking him off these days for swearing or losing his temper. He couldn't talk to her any more.

Robert didn't have a best friend though he'd always wanted one. If his parents had had their children closer together it might have happened, with a brother or sister, but there were these ridiculous age gaps. It was going to be even more ridiculous soon because Mum was pregnant. He'd be fourteen by the time the baby was born, more like its uncle.

He didn't like to think about home life with a new baby around, Mum was quite bad enough already and the world's worst housewife. She wasn't a feminist, going on marches and burning her underwear, she was just plain vague, more interested in reading and playing the piano than looking after the happy home.

They often came back ravenous from school to discover there was nothing in for tea. She'd got stuck in some 'fascinating' biography and forgotten all about food, till the shops were shut. Those nights they all had toast and cornflakes, including Dad. She was vague about the washing too. Assembling a clean set of school clothes on Monday morning was a major achievement. Robert had once set off squeezed into a pair of Ping's knickers, in lieu of underpants.

When he complained, though, Mum just laughed and Dad always took her side, and said they ought to help more.

'Robert? *Robert*! Do you want some tea, lovie?'
Lovie – she was obviously soft-soaping him now,
because of his room. Tea in itself was getting to be an
event because she was tired all the time. It was usually
D.I.Y. these days, with jam and the breadknife. Ping
must have told her about Nick; she was probably
holding forth at this very minute about trespasses
being forgiven. Well, he had his own views on that
and they were going to hear them.

He got up from the wrecked bed and stormed down
the attic stairs.

He was all set to make his speech but when he reached
the kitchen door he decided against it. Dad was home,
much earlier than usual, and he looked furious. Nick
was staring down in disbelief at his red hands and
grizzling. 'That was *hard*,' he sobbed. 'You smacked
me very *hard*, Daddy.'

'I'd have hit you harder than that,' Robert
whispered to Ping, sliding into his seat.

'I'd shut up if I were you,' she whispered back. 'He's
just been thumped for wrecking your room, not that I
approve of corporal punishment.'

'Oh, for heaven's sake, what do you expect Dad to
do? Give him a hundred lines?'

'He's in a *bad mood*,' she hissed. 'I think something's
happened at work.'

Tell me news, not history, thought Robert, hacking
at the loaf. These days work always seemed to depress
his father.

Even at the tea table, frowning over a letter, Jim
Elliott looked like an oversized barn owl. He was tall
and broad with a mop of coarse, crinkly brown hair
that he was always vaguely patting down. These were

his feathers. He had large heavy-lidded eyes that blinked behind thick-rimmed glasses, giving him a wise look, and his hands were huge, 'paws' Ping used to call them. Robert's great comfort, when he was little, had been to fit his tiny hand secretly into Dad's great big one.

Ping was right though, he did look fed up. He was a mild sort of man normally, but he could get into vile tempers if someone caught him on the raw. Robert decided to keep quiet about the mess up in his attic and began to eat his tea in silence.

'What's wrong, Jim?' Mum said, coming through from the back kitchen. 'I thought you'd be pleased about that. We could go tomorrow, couldn't we, if you've not got to work?'

'Tomorrow's fine,' Dad said, but bitterly somehow. 'I'll have all the time in the world for country cottages in a week or so.'

Mum looked at him and pulled a certain face and he looked back. They didn't need to say any words to each other. It sometimes made Robert feel shut out, this telepathy between them.

Dad growled, 'They've sacked Fred.'

'Fred? But why?' Robert wanted to know. Fred Greaves was great and Dad's best mate at work; the whole family liked him.

'Oh, the usual thing, cutting down etc, not enough work to go round. You know the line everyone's taking. It'll be me next. And they're arguing over how much money to give him, needless to say.'

'I hate Steeles,' Nick announced.

'It's wrong to hate people,' Ping informed him.

Steeles was a firm of architects in town and Dad had worked for them for years. Robert thought they were

6

cheats. They'd once promised Dad a partnership and he'd actually paid some cash over. But he was still waiting. That was one of the things about Dad, he wasn't a fighter. He let people get away with murder because he thought everything would come right in the end, and it really irritated Robert. He wouldn't let Steeles ride rough-shod over *him*.

'Surely they couldn't get rid of you, Dad?' he said. 'I mean, who's left if you go?'

'All the Steeles. If there's no work there's no work. Wish I could start up on my own, though.'

'Starting up on his own' was Dad's big dream, like Nick having Hi-Tec sneakers and Robert being handsome. He'd talked about it for as long as they could remember. It didn't seem likely to happen now, though; going on the dole sounded much more probable.

'Anyhow, have you read Aunt Em's letter?' Mum said, proudly putting a plate of jam tarts on the table.

'They look disgusting,' Robert whispered to Ping.

'Shh . . .' she giggled. 'She's pleased with them.'

'Who's Aunt Em?' Nick said, stuffing one down. 'Ugh, this is *burnt*.'

'Well, I think I got the oven a bit hot, lovie. Aunt Em's Grandma's little sister, the one who married Uncle Donald and went to New Zealand.'

'D'you mean Aunt Meanie?' Robert said.

'Why's she called Aunt Meanie?' Nick had removed the tart from his mouth and was wiping his hands on the tablecloth.

'Well, she's dead rich, but she never spends any of it.'

'She knitted Dad a sweater once,' Ping remembered. 'It looked like an old dishcloth and it came down to his knees.'

'*Listen,*' Mum told them, 'and don't be so unkind. She's not as mean as all that. You know that cottage she's got in Wales, the one she's always rented out? Well, she's selling it, but not for a while. It's empty at the moment and she says we can borrow it, for holidays and things.'

Big thrill, Robert was thinking. He'd got a letter in his bag about a school skiing trip but he might as well tear it up if Dad was about to go on the dole. He didn't fancy a holiday in a cottage though, the people at school with country cottages were the flashy ones, dads with personalised number plates and sisters with ponies. Somehow country cottages weren't *them*.

'I want to go to Alton Towers for my holidays,' Nick announced, 'not to a horrible cottage.'

'Well, it might be the only holiday you get,' Dad told him, getting up from the table, 'so I'd stop moaning if I were you.'

'Yes, stop moaning,' Ping repeated. 'These jam tarts are gorgeous, Mum,' she said.

Liar, thought Robert.

'I'll ring this Tom Williams now,' Dad said, 'he's still got a key. Just in case they can meet us there tomorrow.' And he went into the hall.

'Was it the cottage where you went when you were a little girl?' Nick wanted to know. 'Were you naughty?'

'Yes, I was, even naughtier than you.'

'Oh.'

'Is it near the sea, Mum?' Robert said. Dad seemed keen to go to the place so he might as well know all about it. He loved the sea and he'd had this sudden vision of an old stone fisherman's cottage perched high above some lonely beach, with enormous waves breaking over the garden wall. When they were on

8

holiday and reached the sea at last after a long sticky journey, with Nick grizzling and Ping being carsick, he always felt he was taking his first breath, the first breath of his life.

'Near the sea? No, not really, it's more inland, near the hills.'

He felt a stab of disappointment. Not near the sea . . . and *hills* . . . not even mountains. It was going to be boring.

It was Friday. When his father came back from the phone he sounded quite cheerful.

'They were in,' he said, 'and it's all fixed up. They'll meet us there tomorrow, about twelve. I've got a job to do now,' he added suddenly, 'and I want you all in bed early. We should try and get away in good time tomorrow anyhow, to beat the traffic.'

They heard him climb the stairs. After a minute or two the door of his work-room at the back of the house slammed shut. While Mum got Nick into the bath, Ping helped Robert clear up his attic. It was obviously her good deed for the day. Dad had been in already and propped the broken leg up with two bricks.

'Do you feel excited about tomorrow?' she asked him.

'Not really. I think it sounds a bit boring. I wish it was near the sea.'

'I don't mind about that, I just want it to be all on its own, you know, really cut off. Do you think it will be?'

'Dunno. You'll have to ask Mum. She obviously thinks it's OK. Why do you want it to be on its own, though?'

Ping turned red. 'Oh, you know, it'd be . . . well, more romantic somehow. It's so squashed here, all the houses in a row.'

'I know what you mean.' Then he added, 'You'll have to go to chapel there, Ping, it's Wales. They preach for hours and hours in Wales, and you just have to sit there.'

'Oh, that's OK,' she said cheerfully. 'Next time, I'm going to ask if Sally can come too. She'd be interested in all that.'

Why did I go and open my big mouth, Robert thought grumpily, getting into bed.

As he was drifting off, Mum came up to say goodnight. He could still hear his father's radio, down in the work-room.

'Hasn't Dad finished that job yet? What was it, anyhow?'

'Er . . . I'm not quite sure,' she said vaguely. 'He just mentioned that it was a bit tricky. Have a nice night.'

She tucked him in, ruffling the top of his head, and Robert snuggled down. Three floors below, the traffic to Chester roared on. He thought of the silent Welsh hills and felt a twinge of excitement about tomorrow. Anything was better than noisy, smelly Buckden Heath.

It was light when he woke up and the sun poured in through the window, on to Dad's 'job' of the night before. The *Mary Rose*, miraculously restored, stood gay with all its pennants streaming, inviting him to get up and start the journey.

CHAPTER TWO

Nick was always a pain on car journeys and he whinged all the way to Chester. He kept going on about sitting 'on the lion's side' but nobody could work out what he meant.

Dad made good time till they got stuck in a massive traffic jam in a village called Church Stoken, an ancient crumbling place with black and white houses that jutted out over the road. Nick stopped grizzling as the car slowed down, and pointed through the window. 'I *am* on the lion's side,' he said, 'it's *there*.'

They'd drawn level with an old boarded-up chapel set well back from the pavement. In front was a cobbled yard and in the middle of it, mounted on a concrete plinth, was a lion of stone.

It was lying down in a Trafalgar Square position but sideways, as if it liked the sun on its belly, and it had that slight smile which all great cats have; but there was no other gentleness. Something about it made you go on looking. Robert stared at the shaggy head with its great sad eyes. Even though they were stone they still burned with a curious inner life. The tassel on its tail looked real enough to flick away the sparrow that had landed on it. Everyone was looking at it now.

11

'I've seen that before,' Ping said. 'I think it's historic. We came here with school.'

Mum came to life at the word 'historic' and poked about in the glove compartment. She brought out a wadge of screwed-up tissues, some Polos covered with fluff and a book. 'It'll be in this,' and she waved it triumphantly, *The Border Country*. Let's see what it says.'

Robert and Ping exchanged looks and waited for the lecture. 'It belonged to the Parry family,' she said, after a minute or so's flicking through the pages. 'It was a kind of talisman. They carried it round with them, to their battles.'

'But it must weigh a ton.'

'Well, that's what it says here.'

'Who were the Parrys, then?'

'Oh, one of those awful border families who were always fighting with their neighbours. It says here that they claimed to have royal blood.'

'They sound like the Piggotts,' Ping remarked. Old Mr and Mrs Piggott next door didn't like the Elliott children and they banged on the wall if Robert played his tapes too loud. 'You'd think Mrs Piggott was royal,' she added, 'the way she goes on.'

'That's not very Christian, is it?' Robert said smartly.

'Oh, belt up, you,' and Ping pulled her tongue out.

'But how can you tell when you're a king?' Nick wanted to know. 'How do we *get* kings?'

Mum thought about this for a minute, then she said slowly, 'Well, in the olden days, when everyone was living in tribes, it would be the bravest and the cleverest ones who became the leaders.'

'The noblest ones,' added Ping, who loved words.

Across the border the countryside gradually

changed. They'd left the boring main road and struck up into hillier land. The houses weren't in tight orderly villages like the Cheshire ones but in straggly settlements with roads that went nowhere, and hens and sheep wandering about. The houses were different too, white-washed mainly and with knobbly walls. When they passed an unpainted one Robert saw that it was built of great boulders roughly flung together. Rocks littered the desolate moorland and the road ribboned in front of them, white in the sunshine. Sometimes a rock turned into a sheep and scampered away.

The road was getting narrower and narrower and tufts of grass grew in the middle. Dad swerved into a gateway to let a tractor go by and they stopped abruptly. Through the gap Robert saw a small meadow brushed with new green. Above it, the moor sloped up gently to a line of trees. Then there were mountains, a whole range of them, the bluish contours laid on top of each other like paper cut-outs, shimmering slightly in the sun.

They went down a hill and Dad suddenly braked again. 'We're here,' he said, 'there's the phone-box. I think the Williamses have just arrived, too.' An immaculate blue Metro was parked on some grass and in it sat a little grey-haired couple unscrewing a Thermos flask. The Elliotts scrambled out of their dirty old estate car and Mum and Dad went to introduce themselves. Robert and Ping stared at the house.

It was a long white cottage like the ones they'd seen on the way, built right on to the road that sloped sharply down hill, out of sight. The front looked on to a belt of rough trees, the back on to a paddock of grass. There was no mountain view and no sea. Robert

13

sincerely hoped Mum and Dad wouldn't want to look after it for Aunt Em. It would probably be even more boring than Buckden Heath.

Inside, it smelt musty and stale and the cold went right through him. The Williamses had moved out weeks ago, to a bungalow in Colwyn Bay. 'The Aga'll soon warm it up,' Mrs Williams was telling Mum. 'It's lovely in the cold weather, though it's a bit fiddly to light. It's rather an old one.'

'I'm sure it's going to be wonderful,' beamed Mum, but Robert's heart had plummeted. He pictured himself lying for hours on the cold flag-stones trying to light the thing, with Nick jumping up and down on him, Dad away on some job, and Mum making encouraging noises from the sidelines. It was fatal, being the only really practical member of the family.

While Mum was shown the wonders of the Aga he went exploring with Ping. In spite of himself he felt quite excited as he wandered around, it was so very old and the stone walls were amazingly thick. In places they turned into little passages and everything sloped and bulged and creaked.

The tiny sitting room looked on to a ragged garden, bright with daffodils. Ping tried the latch of a door in the corner and peeped out. There was a deafening noise which Robert couldn't identify. First he thought it was water running, then the whirr of some invisible machine. Then he listened again, his ears focussing so hard on the strange new sound they almost hurt him. It was birdsong.

Upstairs there were four dark bedrooms with tiny windows. All of them looked out on to dull trees or dull paddocks and there were no views of anything much. Ping had already bagged a room at the back.

14

'I'm having this one,' she told him, 'because it's not overlooked by that farm. We can get a camp bed in here, too, for Sally. Mum and Dad'll have to have the big one, and Nick'll have to go next door in the tiny room. Yours is the second biggest,' she added generously.

Robert climbed up three steps in to his bedroom. It was a lot larger than Ping's with the bathroom and kitchen underneath. The farm she objected to was represented by half an inch of corrugated iron barn, way up the hill. She was crazy. Being 'spied on' was one of her obsessions. He looked round, noting that the old saggy bed looked most uncomfortable and that a massive wardrobe took up a lot of the floor space. Then he started to pace up and down. Something was puzzling him. In the dust he drew a neat plan, first the ground floor of the cottage, then the upstairs. 'There's something odd about this room,' he told Ping. 'It's only about two thirds as big as it should be. Look.'

She studied the plan and shrugged. 'Well, perhaps the back wall's just extra thick. Some of the downstairs ones are fantastic.' She knocked on it with her knuckles, to demonstrate. 'Ouch! It feels pretty solid to me.'

'Well, if it *is* a wall it's got to be about six feet thick. That's some wall,' Robert said thoughtfully.

'Don't be so boring. Why do you have to make such a mystery of it, anyhow? Old places are always a bit funny.'

The Williamses had gone down to the village to look up some friends. Everyone sat on the grass eating Mum's 'picnic', doorstep sandwiches, half syrup, half marmite. She'd not been able to find anything else.

'Can you remember the house?' Robert said, feeding his to the birds.

'Oh yes, I remember it. I spent a lot of summers here, when I was little. You always remember those holidays best. Do you like it?'

Her voice was wavering and he glanced at her shyly. She was staring across at Aunt Em's cottage with an intense, far-away look in her eyes and she looked a bit sad.

He stared too. The simple old house stood hopefully before them. Someone had left the door open. Under the spring sunshine the scene was white and gold against green; the whitewashed walls were crisscrossed by branches shot with new buds; flowers starred the paddock. And there *were* mountains, though miles away and only glimpsed at through a tiny tree gap, mountains which at noon were losing their blue-black and turning gold under the light. When the fresh breeze dropped for a minute there was an absolute stillness, and the delirium of that marvellous birdsong.

The noises of Buckden Heath, the traffic and the factory hooters, the boats on the canal all came rushing in on him him. This place was better. He said 'It's great, Mum, it'd be great to come in the summer.'

When the Williamses came back Ping asked them about the farm on the hillside but they didn't seem very anxious to talk about it. 'You mean Reg Morgan's place? Well, he's not too friendly, is he, Tom?' Mrs Williams sounded quite embarrassed. 'They'll sell you milk and eggs if you go up there, but there's never much of a welcome. The Morgans keep themselves to themselves.'

'Are there any children?' Mum said.

16

'Yes, a boy, Gareth. He'd be about your age, dear,' Mrs Williams said, looking at Robert. 'Or a bit younger perhaps. His grandma looks after him, and his Dad. He – his mother died. A long time ago, that was.'

Robert pricked his ears up. So there was a boy up the road, somebody of his own age, a solitary boy probably. He felt solitary, too, even in the middle of this mad family. Gareth could become the best friend he'd always secretly hoped for.

Mum must have read his mind. 'Perhaps we could get him down here in the summer,' she suggested, 'if he's Robert's age? It'd be nice for these three.'

But Mrs Williams poured cold water on that. 'I really wouldn't bother with that family,' she said briskly. 'Er, should I take you through the Aga procedure again? It'd be such a pity if you couldn't get it going.'

End of subject, thought Robert, watching her totter across the grass. Funny, though, there was obviously more to it than she'd said. He was going to keep his ears open.

For now there was that massive wall in his room to examine. 'Dad,' he said. 'Do you think my bedroom's been divided up or something? It's not nearly as big as it should be. Look at the gable end.'

His father stared up at it critically, and grinned. 'You're a cleverclogs, aren't you? Yes, you're right. According to Aunt Em, one bit was filled up with rubble years ago, and plastered over. Mum said she got a builder to have a go at it once, to make a bit more room, but it was all solid.'

'Why fill it in, though?'

'It was probably very damp, it's a north-facing wall. It'd have been much easier to fill it in a bit, you know, thicken it. Why? Were you thinking of taking a

17

hammer to it or something? I don't think you'd get very far.'

'Course I wasn't,' Robert muttered, but he felt himself going red. That's just what he *had* been thinking.

While the others were saying goodbye to the Williamses and having a last look round, Robert slipped off. There was a gate at the end of the garden which led into a meadow. He went through it and started to walk.

When he was through the tangle of thick trees that bordered the grass he could see much more. The first field was flat but the second one sloped up quite sharply and eventually turned into rough common, separated from the rest by a rotten fence. He crawled through it then stood up panting. The cottage was now a mere white flash down below and he was knee-deep in gorse bushes. The mountains ringed two thirds of the horizon and looked much nearer, even though they were still miles away.

He bent down to scratch his leg and something licked his hand. A little dog was at his feet, a black and white mongrel with half a tail and one eye hideously sealed up with a fleshy growth. It was the ugliest dog he'd ever seen but its single eye was bright with love and when he scratched its ears its tail whirred like an engine.

He knelt down and stroked it properly and it stopped yelping to listen to his voice. There was no sound at all now, not even birdsong. Then it was drowned by something much louder, a sharp cracking noise and something exploding near his feet. The dog barked and ran off, and Robert looked up. Someone was staring at him from over the broken-down fence.

18

He stared back. The boy was a lot shorter than him and rather thick-set, with a round red face and a fringe of heavy black hair. His dark eyes were fixed stonily on Robert and his mouth was all screwed up. He wore old jeans and a red sweater with reindeers on.

Robert noticed how large his hands were. One shot out suddenly from his pocket to grab the whining dog by the collar. In the other was a small pistol.

'What the hell d'you think you're playing at?' Robert shouted. Now he was sure the boy had fired at him, he felt frightened, and he thrust his hands into the pockets of his jeans, to stop them shaking.

'I said what on earth –'

But the boy didn't even look at him. 'Come on, Rags,' he whistled to the dog and they set off, up the moor. Then Robert heard the car horn bleeping from down the fields. They were waiting for him.

'I'm telling my Dad,' he yelled after the boy. 'You can't just go firing guns at people.'

'Do what you sodding well like.' The thin clipped Welsh voice floated back to him through the gorse, then the car horn bleeped again.

Robert scrambled back through the fence and ran down to the cottage. Dad was looking out for him, jangling the keys.

'Sorry, I didn't think you'd be ready yet. There's a boy up the hill.'

'Hop in.' Mr Elliott hadn't heard. He was too preoccupied, thinking about the route home, and Nick was grizzling. Mum was trying to divert him with sticky Polos.

'Move up, then,' he told Ping. 'Give me a bit more room, you two are taking up the whole seat.'

'What's it like up there, then? Find anything

19

interesting?' Dad turned the key in the ignition, revved, and drove off slowly.

Robert hesitated. 'No, not really, there's a great view though. Those mountains look really close.'

'I knew you'd like it,' Mum said dreamily. 'We had picnics up on that common, gorgeous picnics.'

'Did you have syrup sandwiches?' Ping whispered.

'Now don't be horrible to your poor old mother. They were all right.'

'I do like it, Mum, honestly, I want to come back,' she said. 'Could we come next weekend? Could I ask Sally?'

Robert groaned.

'Look,' said Dad, 'Wait a minute, what's the big hurry? You are going to have the whole summer here. Lucky you lot. I'll be working, or else I'll be down at the job centre every day. People camp out there these days.'

'I like that big fire-place with the beam,' Ping said.

'I like my tiny little room.'

But Robert didn't speak. He wasn't going to tell them about the boy with the gun. Not now, not yet. They all seemed so happy.

CHAPTER THREE

In the weeks that followed he thought about the boy a lot. What could have been bugging him, to go after somebody with a gun? Robert had hardly said two words to him, yet he'd felt the hate.

Was it an anti-English thing? People who owned holiday cottages in Wales sometimes had them burned down. Could it be that? He wasn't to know that the cottage belonged to somebody else and was going to be sold anyhow, that Dad could hardly pay his bills and would probably lose his job. He might be less hostile if he knew the inside story.

Robert had had thoughts about Aunt Em's too, thoughts that surprised him. As the grey rain bucketed down over the grey town and Chester Road turned into a riot of orange cones with heavy equipment dragged in, ready for the digging of a new gas main, the little white cottage became a quiet sunshiny clearing in his mind, a place he dipped into, like a secret pool. He found himself wanting to go back, just for the peace of it.

In May, school half term, they did, for a whole week. Dad was on 'monthly pay' now which meant Steeles could ask him to go with only four weeks' notice. It sounded bad.

'This is a *paid* holiday, isn't it Dad?' Ping said anxiously. But her father merely grunted and disappeared upstairs, pretending not to hear.

'Of course he's not being *paid*,' Robert muttered in her ear. 'They're trying to show him the door. Surely you understand that much?' It was happening all over the place now, half the people in his class had parents out of work; not that it made Dad's position any better. He was often short-tempered these days – and no wonder. It was a great moment to be losing your job, with another baby about to be born. Perfect Elliott timing, as usual.

As they drove to the cottage Robert tried to concentrate on the good things, a whole week at Aunt Em's with nothing to do except what he wanted, fine weather for exploring round, with a bit of luck, and that peculiar old wall to go at, up in his bedroom. He always had a 'project' in hand because he got bored otherwise, and his cottage project was to penetrate the wall. He was going to tackle Gareth Morgan too, if he got half a chance.

It was nearly dark when they arrived but there was enough light left to see that the countryside was completely different from when they'd first come here on that bare March day. Everything was lush and green now and the growth was so thick everywhere that all the views had gone. Even the mountains through the gateway were mere bluey-green smudges, lost behind trees that had shaken out their summer branches in a fanfare of wild leaves.

The cottage itself now stood in the middle of a jungle, knee-deep in grass. Creepers and climbing roses, too heavy for their supports, had fallen away from the walls and lay on the ground in a tangle. It was weeks since the Williamses had cut the paddock for the last time, packed up their secateurs and gone back to Colwyn Bay.

They stared for a minute, disappointed by the neglect of it all, then Ping shouted, 'Look, it's all right, smoke's coming out of one of the chimneys! And someone *has* been here, the grass is all flat.'

Her parents exchanged one of their secret looks, then Dad did something they liked. 'Here,' he said, fishing in his pocket and bringing out a key, 'you go and unlock. Nick's fast asleep. I'd like to get him straight into bed if I can.'

It was warm in the kitchen because somebody had come in and lit the Aga. On the table was a blue jug full of milk and a large brown loaf. Robert found an old envelope with scribbles on it. 'For milk tomorrow call at Morgans,' he read. 'Firewood, coal etc. in outhouse. Yours and oblige, D. Preece.'

Dad said 'Can we come in?' He was standing at the top of the kitchen steps with the sleeping Nick over his right shoulder and his big left hand in Mum's small one. Robert remembered that scene for always, his father's bulk blotting out the last light from the garden as they stood together in the doorway looking down.

'That loaf looks good,' Mum said. 'I think I'll brew up before we do the beds. Anyone want a cup?'

'Who's D. Preece, Mum?' Ping asked, reading the envelope.

'A lady from the village who used to come and clean round for Mrs Williams. What a good job she left that milk. I'd forgotten to bring any.'

The two children pulled faces at each other. What else would she have forgotten? Food? Bedding? Toilet paper? The nearest shop was miles away.

23

'Grandma was friends with some Preeces in the village,' she went on. 'It's probably the same family. The D's for "Dilys", if I've got the right person.'

Nick had been smuggled into bed brilliantly by Dad, without actually waking up. After mugs of tea and hunks of Dilys's loaf the others were packed off too. Neither of them minded; there was something special about going to bed in a different house for the very first time, particularly in an ancient house like this with its bumps and its creaks and its bulging walls.

'Wonder if it's got any ghosts?' Ping said dreamily, drifting round in her nightdress and poking vaguely at the double thick wall in Robert's room. She always took hours getting ready for bed, it drove Dad wild.

'Don't believe in them,' Robert told her, getting comfortable in his sleeping bag. 'Anyhow, I thought it wasn't "Christian" to be interested in ghosts.'

'Oh *yes*, there are ghosts and things in the Bible.'

'Well, there are bound to be mice,' he said wickedly. 'So I'd get into bed quick if I were you.' But Ping didn't hear.

'I think any ghosts here are *friendly*,' she stated firmly. 'This house has got a nice feel to it. Though I suppose a lot of people must have died here,' she added, with a slight frown.

'And been born.' Robert was thinking of Mum who, as the birth of the new baby got near, was gradually starting to resemble the Incredible Hulk. 'Shut the door when you go out,' he called after her, as she wafted away. 'And watch out for the mice.'

Ping was right though, Aunt Em's did have a good 'feel' to it. They were going to be happy here; pity they'd only got a week.

He lay awake for a long time that night, unused to

the deep quietness of the countryside. A couple of cars rattled past and an owl hooted; otherwise there was total silence.

The owl rather excited him. He'd heard them on radio programmes but this was real, it was out there in the fields, hunting.

A real owl. Wrapped round in the enormous silence he slept at last.

When he opened his eyes he smelt toast burning. Mum was up, anyway. Nick burst in and crawled under the bed, poking at him through the lumpy mattress. 'Get up, you. Daddy sent me.'

'Leave my things alone or I'll thump you.'

Nick was rummaging about in the open suitcase and his tools were at the bottom, all ready for attacking the wall. It'd be just like him to find them, and go prattling to Dad.

'What's this?'

'Clear *out*! I want to get dressed. And shut the door after you!' Robert hated getting up.

Breakfast was more or less finished by the time he got downstairs and so was the milk. He upended the blue jug and got half an inch for his cornflakes. '*Mum!* You might have saved me a bit.'

'A drop, lovie. It's a drop when it's liquid.'

'Well, so what? There's none left.' He felt famished, too. Why couldn't she have brought some milk from home? She was ridiculous.

'Don't be insolent, Robert.' Dad had appeared in the doorway with a hod of coke for the Aga. According to Ping, it had gone out in the night and taken him hours to re-light; his cheerful first-day-of-the-hols mood had quite obviously evaporated already.

'I'm not. I just wanted some milk for my cereal, that's all. It's a perfectly reasonable request. Any normal family —'

'I said shut *up*. Here,' and Dad dug into his pocket. 'Go up to that farm for some. You could get eggs too, then we'll have something for dinner.'

Robert didn't need asking twice. Here was a golden opportunity to see the boy again, and tackle him about the gun. He took the money and shot upstairs to get his anorak.

Five minutes later he was walking up the lane with Dilys's jug. Mum had insisted on that even though he'd argued that it was bound to come in bottles. Milk from the cow in an old blue jug was part of Mum's little dream world.

He soon spotted Morgans' up on the left, a clutter of buildings at the top of a track that curved over the brow of a hillside. The sign on the road said 'Milk and Eggs' in runny red letters on a white-painted board. It was muddy underfoot and there was a strong smell of manure.

'Ugh, that smells like poohs!' Nick had appeared suddenly, out of nowhere, and as Robert stood and glared at him Ping came into view at the bottom of the lane and started running up the track to join them.

'What have you two come for?'

'To see what it's like. To see that boy. It's that farm, isn't it?'

'Yes it is, but . . . for heaven's *sake*. You didn't need to tag along.'

Ping stared at him curiously. 'Why shouldn't we,' she said, 'and why did you just go off, without saying anything?'

'Oh come on,' he said irritably, 'and nobody *say* anything. We'll just get the milk and come back.'

They walked up the track in silence, looking at the rubbish everywhere. Holes in the hedges had been filled in with pieces of corrugated iron and old doors, and the farmhouse itself stood in a desolate yard with grass growing up between the flagstones. Bits of brick and animal dung lay all over the place and the gate was tied to its post with a piece of rope. It looked as if nobody had swept or tidied the place for years.

As they went up to the door it started raining. Nick began grizzling. 'I don't like that smell,' he whimpered, 'and I'm cold. I want to go home.'

Robert gave Ping the jug and picked him up, then he banged on the door. It sounded horribly loud in the deserted yard and a dog barked somewhere, far away. Then the door was opened by an ancient old woman. Nick stiffened and turned his face away. He'd got a real thing about 'witches'. What if he said something?

'Please could we have some milk, and a dozen eggs?' Robert said nervously and Ping held the blue jug out. The witch looked about a hundred, she had leathery brown skin and very bright blue eyes. But she smiled at them, revealing a single tooth in an otherwise empty mouth; then she beckoned them inside, talking Welsh to them very fast.

'She talks foreign,' Nick whispered, looking round the dark stuffy kitchen, and sniffing. 'She's been baking cakes too. Wish I could have one.'

'Shut *up*,' Robert hissed at him, putting him on the floor and looking round himself.

The first thing he saw was a gun, not a pistol like Gareth's but a large shotgun hanging over the fireplace. The butt and barrel gleamed in the electric light,

27

it looked as if it was the only cared-for thing in the place. Otherwise the kitchen was as ramshackle as the farmyard.

The old woman took the jug and motioned them on to an ancient settee. They had to remove newspapers and rubbish before they could sit down: it was worse than at home, and in his efforts to push Ping along the cushions and secure a place for himself, Nick actually fell off the end.

'Ow!' he complained loudly. 'Move up, and let me get on.' Then somebody laughed spitefully out of a dark corner. It was the boy.

'Oh, hi,' Ping said brightly. 'We didn't see you there. Mrs Preece left a note to say you sold milk, and we've run out. It's a bit typical of Mum, now she's having a baby. It can make you lose your memory you know.'

'Oh yeah?' said the boy, staring. Inside, Robert willed her to stop rabbiting on. The boy would be sneering at her, sneering at Mum. He was still wearing the dirty red sweater with the reindeers on and his face had that same nasty screwed-up look.

The old woman had filled their jug with milk and put it on the table with another one. She gabbled some Welsh to Gareth and he slid off his chair and fetched four mugs. Then a baking tray was produced out of an iron range and the contents scooped on to a plate. Soon the three Elliotts were sitting in a row on the lumpy settee, drinking milk and munching hot buttered buns. Gareth went back to the corner with his, and opened a comic.

Now there was food inside him Nick had cheered up considerably. The old woman got an old sweet tin down from a shelf and tipped a heap of buttons on to the table, and he started to arrange them in neat rows on the tablecloth. He liked buttons, Gran had a button tin too. 'Look!' and he grabbed her hand. 'Look at this great big gold one, it's got a ship on.'

'It's no good talking to her,' the Welsh boy said peevishly. 'She doesn't speak English.'

'Well you needn't be so foul about it, need you?' Ping said belligerently. 'He's only five, you know.'

'Why don't you just drop dead?'

Ping turned bright red and took a step towards him. *Don't Ping*, Robert pleaded silently, for heaven's sake *don't*. She had a fiendish temper when something really annoyed her and she always stuck up for Nick.

They were glaring at each other silently when something drove into the yard and a car door banged. Gareth's gran dropped the buttons as if they were red hot and shuffled off through a door, then they heard water running in a sink. The door opened and Rags bounded in, sniffing at the three Elliotts and jumping up at Gareth.

An enormous man stood in the doorway, tall and thick-set with a small head that looked as if it belonged to a much thinner body. The remains of his hair were curly and black and in his swollen red face his dark eyes looked like two tiny currants. There was something very hard about his mouth.

He stared at them all in silence, at the plate of cake crumbs, the button box. Then words came in torrents, all in Welsh but obviously about them. Gareth's comic was snatched away and he was shoved in the direction of a pair of mud-caked boots that stood by the back door on a piece of newspaper. Rags was there already, whining to be let out.

Morgan flung the door open and kicked the boots

29

into the yard. As Rags ran out he aimed a kick at him too, and the dog ran off whimpering.

'How *could* you –' Ping started, but Robert dug his fingernails into her arm as Gareth pushed past, his face scarlet. Morgan had started on Gran now but she simply went on swilling dishes, answering through her back in a weary kind of voice that suggested they'd been through scenes like this many times before.

'Come on,' Robert whispered, and they all got to their feet. 'Could you tell us what we owe you for this milk, please?' He wasn't going to bother with eggs, they could have cornflakes for dinner, for all he cared.

'Afternoons are the best time to come,' Morgan told him. 'We're busy mornings. 50p you owe me.'

'Thanks,' Robert said, handing over the money. They didn't exactly look busy and he felt like saying so. Ping wanted to say 'You're the most horrible person I've ever met,' as she walked past him. Nick did say 'I hate that awful fat man,' but not before he'd slammed the door on them. Gareth was in the yard, scraping mud off the filthy boots with an old knife. As they went through the gate he turned his face away.

It took a long time to get down the track because Robert had to balance the milk jug and it was slippery underfoot. When they reached the lane he stopped and looked back at the farm. Gareth was standing halfway up the slope now, looking down at them. He stepped back into the hedge when he saw Robert.

Dad said they were exaggerating about Reg Morgan. 'Nobody's as bad as that,' he told them.

'He was, he was foul,' Ping spluttered. 'He kicked the dog.'

'He'd have kicked Gareth too, if we'd not been there.'

'It smelt horrible, as well.'

'Well, Mrs Williams did warn us about him,' Mum said. 'Never mind, we can always get milk in the village, even though it'll be in bottles.' She was tickled pink about the jug.

'Gareth's got a much older brother,' Dad said. 'According to the Williamses he ran away from home and got a job in Cardiff. He's not been back to that farm for years. I thought it might be just gossip but if he's as bad as you're making out it sounds as if his father drove him to it.'

'They'd got a piano in their kitchen,' Nick said. 'I think it must've belonged to his mummy that died.'

'It was covered with rubbish,' Ping told them. 'It didn't look as if anyone played it much.'

'The boy's musical, though,' Mum said, 'Mrs Williams told me. That's one reason I hoped you could make friends with him. There's an old piano in the barn. We could have brought it in here and played a bit together. It's about time I did some practising, I'm rusty.'

'You can die having babies,' Nick announced dramatically, pursuing his own private train of thought and eyeing Mum's bump.

'Look, *nobody's* going to die,' Dad said. 'Anyhow, we were talking about that poor sad man up the road.'

'He's not poor,' Ping told him indignantly. 'The farm's a real tip but I bet he's got millions stashed away. Rich people often live in tips.'

'And why do you say he's "sad"?' Robert wanted to know.

'Well, his wife died when the two children were young, in fact Gareth could only have been a baby. After that he just opted out, apparently, lost his interest in everything, apart from the bottle. He's a heavy drinker, according to the Williamses. And he's a great one for feuding with his neighbours over bits of land, too. So we'd better watch it.' Dad smiled, but only with his mouth. He clearly didn't much like what he'd heard about Gareth's father.

'Well, since this cottage isn't even ours he can't very well get on to us, can he?' Robert pointed out.

'True. All I'm saying is that it's obviously better to keep out of his way, if he's as awkward as that.'

Mum and Ping were organising a shopping expedition into Llandewi, the nearby market town, on the afternoon bus. Nick was going with them. He liked the shops, and he usually managed to wangle a bit of spending money out of his mother. Robert definitely *wasn't* going. He hated shopping and it would be a good opportunity to start on the wall, providing his father went out of earshot for a bit.

His mother had brought enough food in her overnight cardboard box for chips and baked beans. He peeled spuds at the sink while Ping poked about the kitchen looking for plates and knives and forks. Nick had discovered that he could keep his feet warm in the bottom of the Aga and Mum had kicked her shoes off and put hers in too. They laughed as their bare toes met.

Mum got on his nerves sometimes, the way she forgot everything, and Dad had these sudden bursts of ill-temper. But it was all so trivial, compared with the Morgans. Nobody was unhappy; no-one had died.

As he sliced the potatoes and made his special 'slim-Jim' chips that everybody liked, Robert kept seeing Gareth's face bent over those muddy boots and afterwards how he'd stared sadly after them, down the track.

CHAPTER FOUR

An old green bus rattled up to the house at 2 o'clock and Mum, Ping and Nick scrambled on. Dad had offered to drive them to Llandewi himself but Mum was a romantic. She wanted to do the bumpy bus ride across the moors again, just as she had when she was a little girl.

'It looks like the same bus to me,' Robert said, noticing big rust patches.

'Well, it goes,' Mum said loyally. 'Don't be rude, otherwise we won't bring any food back.'

'Will she remember, though?' he asked Dad, as they went inside.

'I made a list and I gave it to Ping. Keep your fingers crossed.'

Aunt Em had always been a great one for going to country furniture sales and the stone barn next to the cottage was crammed with junk. 'She said we could take our pick of what's in here,' Dad told him, opening the door, 'and I'd quite like to get that piano inside, for your mother. We'll need a hand with it, though. Perhaps I'll wander down to the village and find this Mrs Preece. She might have a strapping son to spare. Do you want to come?'

'Er, no, thanks. I'll think I'll stay here and sort my

bedroom out.' His actual plan was to have a proper look at that old wardrobe. With luck, it could provide cover for his wall project, like the wooden vaulting horse in the famous escape story. Inside that horse some men had dug a tunnel and escaped from a prison camp in World War 2.

The minute Dad had disappeared down the lane, he went up to his bedroom and shut the door. There was a crude lock on it already, a hasp that fitted over an iron ring secured with a wooden peg. He'd have to find a proper bolt but the peg would do for now. He sat on the floor and stared at the old wardrobe. Fortunately for him it was positioned in the exact middle of the 'false' wall which was where he wanted it. But before he could get any further the back had to come off.

After a lot of tugging and heaving he managed to get it far enough out from the wall to squeeze behind with his screwdriver. The back – a single piece of reddish timber that gave off a curious perfumed smell – was held in place with a series of large brass screws. Robert removed them carefully and put them in his pocket.

As the last one slid out the whole piece of wood slipped down and crushed his toes. Swearing under his breath, he lugged it across the room and pushed it under his bed. Quite a big piece stuck out, though, so he covered it up with an old 'peg' rug that he'd noticed on the landing outside. Aunt Em obviously had a passion for these, there was one in nearly every room. They were made from pieces of sacking and scraps of what look like ancient men's suits, all brown and black and navy blue. People had pegged them in the old days, according to Mum, when there was no TV.

Now the wardrobe had no back it was bound to rock

35

slightly but nobody was likely to go pushing at it. Anyhow that was a risk he'd got to take. He manoeuvred it back into its original position and opened the door. Then he pulled his shoes off and climbed inside.

In front of him was the cold white plaster; behind him his room, with tools scattered over the floor. He took a pencil from his pocket and drew a rough circle on the white. One day he'd crawl into the secret room through a hole hidden by Aunt Em's wardrobe. In a way he didn't care if the space did prove empty, just as long as he got through.

He hopped out again, climbed back with his big hammer, and swung it at the wall. In the empty house the crash felt ear-splitting and a big lump of plaster fell on the wardrobe floor, crumbling as it fell and revealing another skin of pinkish cement, scored with something sharp. Tiny red insects scurried over it into the safe darkness under the white outer crust. Robert squashed half a dozen with his finger.

In the lane outside a dog was barking. He went over to the window and saw a flash of red go by. There was nobody in sight by the time he'd run downstairs and opened the front door, and he was puzzled. The road that sloped down the hill went straight for quite a distance. How could anyone have got out of sight so quickly?

Then the dog yelped again, at the back this time. He ran upstairs again and looked through Ping's window, just in time to see Gareth's legs disappearing over the paddock wall, and Rags leaping after him.

Downstairs he scribbled on a scrap of paper and pinned it to the back door. 'Gone for a walk, back soon.'

He tried not to make a noise but his sneakers felt loud swishing through the wet grass and he dislodged a couple of big stones as he climbed over the wall. He crouched right down in case Gareth had heard the clatter and looked back but the wind was up, making an ocean sighing in the big trees, drowning the smaller noises of boys and dogs. Robert followed at a distance, keeping in the shadow of the hedge.

He saw Gareth stop at the barbed wire and sit down under an enormous chestnut tree. In the wind its creamy flowers streamed away like snow. Robert stood by the hedge uncertainly but the dog had seen him and came limping down the field to give him a lick.

'Here, Rags!' the other boy said sharply and the mongrel went back, nosing into an old canvas rucksack that he'd thrown on to the grass. The boy took an apple out of his pocket and bit into it, staring across the moors to the distant line of mountains, willing Robert to speak.

'What are you doing in this field?' he said at last. 'It belongs to my Aunt Em. You're trespassing.'

Gareth shifted away from the fence a few inches, and moved his rucksack. 'No I'm not, not now. Anyhow, anybody can come through here, it's a right of way. You ask your auntie.'

'I knew that.'

'Why d'you say it, then? You thick or something?'

Robert felt stupid; he'd simply said the first thing that had come into his head. But he'd got the bit between his teeth now and he wasn't going to let the boy go. 'Why did you shoot that gun at me, that air pistol?'

'I never.'

'You big liar, you *did*. You pointed it straight at me. It might have . . . I could have lost an eye.'

Gareth flushed scarlet and chucked the apple core away. 'Just felt like firing it, didn't I? I shot past you, anyhow, any fool could see that.'

'Oh, that's OK, is it, shooting *past* somebody? Was it your idea of a joke or something? You must be off your rocker.'

'Now you listen to me,' the boy said threateningly, spitting the words out. 'We don't like people like you round here, nobody invited you to come.'

'What do you mean, "people like us"? You don't know us, you know nothing at all about us. You –'

'Well I do, *see*? People like your father I mean, people with a load of money buying up our land so that folk round here can't have it. *Huh.*' He spat into the grass and pushed the dog away from the rucksack, buckling it up quickly. Rags was barking wildly now, trying to get at something inside.

'You leave my father out of it. You're talking crap. For a start, we've not got lots of money and we're certainly not buying that cottage. My father's about to lose his job if you must know. Mum's Aunt Em owns the cottage and she's putting it up for sale soon. We're just using it for the holidays, that's all.'

'Bully for you,' sneered Gareth. 'My dad's not had a holiday for ten years. That's what it's like to be a farmer. Half our village is holiday homes now, it sends the prices up so that local people can't buy them. People don't earn enough round here. Think that's fair, do you? Nearly everyone we know's out of work, then you come, throwing your weight about.'

'I've *told* you,' Robert said again. 'It's *not* our house, we're just –'

38

'And any road,' Gareth interrupted, 'I'm not trespassing, all this was our land, once.'

'Like when?'

'Years ago. It was, though.'

Now it was Robert's turn to sneer. 'Well, Aunt Em owns it now. She was born in that cottage and she's eighty three.'

'*Your Aunt Em*,' Gareth spat at him, as if the name were filthy. 'Don't tell me about her, she's a mean old bag she is, she watches her money all right.'

'Yes, she's like your dad,' Robert said daringly. 'I've heard all about him, trying to cheat people out of their bits of land. Sounds marvellous.'

They'd both stood up at the same moment, and Gareth's face was thrust right up against Robert's, sweaty and red. Both raised their fists. Then, through the trees, they heard Dad's voice. Rags was still scrabbling at the rucksack, the smell of something inside it was clearly driving him wild. Gareth saw Robert looking down at him and kicked the dog hard. 'Leave *off*!'

'Better go, hadn't you? Daddy's calling,' he muttered sarcastically. 'Anyhow, I wouldn't stay a night in your aunt's cottage if you paid me. Someone was murdered in it once.'

Robert stared at him. The boy had obviously said it to scare him and yet the thought chilled him. He saw that damp white wall in his mind, the wall he was going to penetrate, under the cover of Aunt Em's old wardrobe. The murder could have been in that very room.

'Come on, Rags,' and Gareth swung the rucksack on to his shoulder and set off up the moor. Dad called again and Robert started off down the field, very deliberately, but after a minute or so he turned and crept back to the great chestnut tree.

It was broad enough to hide him completely and he stood there, peeping round the trunk to see where Gareth was going. He was walking rapidly, the dog at his heels, towards the line of purplish hills. Then, after a while he seemed to move left. Robert started to climb up into the tree. He was soon well up into the branches and Gareth now only a red blodge striking across the moor.

He was puzzled because there simply seemed nowhere to go. The land looked desolate and uncultivated with no sign of human life at all. The wind had dropped now, and the only thing that moved was a big grey bird that wheeled above him silently. He stared at it, wondering what it was, feeling his ignorance of country things.

And in that second Gareth and Rags disappeared. When Robert's eyes came down to the horizon again it was quite empty. He thought he heard sheep somewhere but the glaring white stones that littered the boggy foreland were too still. The boy and his dog had vanished.

CHAPTER FIVE

Mum was in high holiday mood when they got back, full of the trip to Llandewi and her memories of childhood holidays, and of the new Welsh Museum they'd made out of the old fire station. She kept going off at tangents as she remembered different things, and the precious carrier loads of shopping sat unbroached on the kitchen table.

It was hours since the baked beans and chips and Robert felt hollow. In the end he organised tea himself and set everything out on plates. Mum seemed to have bought up the entire contents of the local bakery and not much else, fruit cake, sponge cake, scones, doughnuts and three different kinds of bread. It suited him. He felt in a mood for pigging it.

'This all looks wonderfully unhealthy, dear,' Dad said, surreptitiously adding a hunk of cheese, apples and half a jar of Marmite.

'Well, they were so nice in the shop. We just got carried away.'

'*You* did,' Pink said severely. 'I'm not having any of that, too much sugar's bad for you. They're not allowed sugar at Sally's. Can I have this end of the table? I want to start my scrapbook.'

'Oh, don't be such a bore,' Robert said, through a

41

mouthful of scone. 'You've got the whole week to do that. It's just typical of your school to give you holiday work. We wouldn't do it at our place, we'd all go on strike.'

Ping ignored him and arranged her museum post-cards very neatly in the scrapbook they'd bought in Woolworth's, before glueing them into position and unscrewing her italic pen. She adored school projects and she always got brilliant marks for them. Part of it was her beautiful handwriting. He watched enviously as she wrote a flowing heading, *THE PARRYS AND THE MORGANS – WAR RAGES*.

'The Morgans? Which Morgans? And what do you mean, *war*?'

'Oh, not real war, just squabbling, but war sounds better. There was a lot in the museum about all those fights the tribes had on the border, and these two seem to have been the main families, round here.'

'Mmm, well, it fits,' Robert said thoughtfully, looking at her postcards. 'The Morgans don't seem to have changed much either. They're still pretty awful.' Not just the father but that lying, bullying son of his. He'd tasted it first hand now.

'It won't be the same Morgans, lovie,' Mum said, dabbing at Nick's nose, to remove a large blob of jam. 'Morgan's a very common Welsh name, it's like Smith or Brown in England.'

'Well, I *bet* it's them,' Robert told her, and so belligerently that she looked at him in some surprise.

'Anyhow, they more or less wiped the Parrys out,' Ping informed him, refilling her italic pen, 'and I think it's a shame, they were obviously *wonderful* people;' and she wrote, *The Great Parry Lion* with a complicated flourish.

'*That* was my best thing,' Nick said, pointing at one of the postcards and depositing a fingerful of jam on the precious scrapbook.

'Get off, get *off*. This is for *school*.'

'Now, now,' Mrs Elliott said mildly, wiping at the page and making the mess worse.

'Oh, *Mum*.'

'That was real gold,' Nick went on. 'It was worth a million pounds.'

The huge signet ring on the postcard was said to be *9th century, possibly the ring of Daniel 'the Great Leader'*. It looked like a fairytale gold nugget. Cut deep into it was a lion's head, not the peaceful stone cat of Church Stoken but a wild forest beast, its mouth open in a roar. The same mark was cut on to two small gold urns, in another picture.

'Those look like funerary urns to me,' Dad said.

'D'you mean for putting dead people in?'

'Well, their ashes.'

'Ugh,' said Nick. 'Why didn't they just bury them in a hole, like we buried Granddad Elliott?'

'I can tell you that,' Mum said. 'There was a big thing about it, on the wall in the museum. When the Parrys declined . . . you know, weren't the *best* any more, they became . . . sort of gypsies, going from place to place. And they started burning their dead, like real gypsies used to. In some countries the gypsies still have funerals by burning their caravans.'

'So the Parrys weren't rich for ever and ever?' Nick said.

'No. It doesn't sound like it.'

'But when they died, how did they –'

'What about a bath, Nick? This Aga's been on all day, thanks to me, and the water's sizzling.'

Robert knew why Dad was removing Nick from the scene. He'd be on about corpses and coffins all night otherwise and Mum, in her enthusiasm to enlarge his education, would go on answering his questions, then wonder why he woke up with nightmares. There was nobody quite like his mother, but Dad was wiser.

'What about this house, Mum?' he said suddenly, when the kitchen door had shut behind them. He was looking at her very closely. She never lied, so did she know about the murder? And had she kept quiet about it, all this time?

But her face was blank. 'What about it, lovie?'

'Well, has it got – you know, a *history* or anything?'

She shrugged. 'Not that I've heard. It's very old, of course, and not the first house to be built on this site, Aunt Em told us that. So it's seen a lot of history in its own way. But, well, I'm sure there's nothing special about it, it's just an old cottage. Why?'

'I only wondered.'

'I've told you, I think it's a *good* house,' Ping murmured, bent over her italic writing. 'It's got a good feel.' And she wrote, *The lion mark has been found on all the household objects shown below, Plates, Goblets, Spoons* . . .

'Eggcups, don't forget eggcups, teapots –'

'Clear *off*, Robert!'

'I am, I am, I'm going upstairs.'

'Hang on,' Mum said, fishing in a carrier bag and pulling something out from underneath a plastic pack of potatoes. 'I bought something for you in Llandewi, at the Oxfam stall. Here, it's out of date but it is one of those lovely old ones.'

Robert slid the folded sheet out of its brown paper. It was an OS map of the Llandewi area on linen cloth, beautifully shaded to show the contours of the hills. He loved maps and he held it to his nose. It smelt wonderful. 'Thanks Mum, it's brilliant.'

When he got upstairs he shut his door and locked it with the peg, then he sat on the bed and looked all round. Ping was right, Aunt Em's cottage did have a good 'feel'. In three hundred years loads of people must have died in it but that was nothing. Murder was another matter but there was no sinister atmosphere in this old place. Gareth Morgan was a liar, just out to scare him.

He unfolded his map and spread it out on the floor. As he pulled the curtains across, he saw the boy walking slowly up the road with Rags trotting wearily at his heels. He looked tired too, and he was dragging his feet, as if he'd walked for miles, over hard tracks.

Robert snapped the light off and peered out. The owl called again, then he heard another voice, a sharp volley of Welsh words, Morgan calling his son. *Gareth*! The only word he recognised echoed shrill and staccato round the sleeping fields. The boy started to run and the dog limped after him.

On the map Robert found Chester and the Dee Estuary, then Llandewi and their own village Groeyurgoch, slightly north of it. Aunt Em's cottage was a minute black rectangle on a minor road that ran between two unnamed hamlets.

Away from the coast the towns and villages got scarcer and a long line of mountains went from East to West, flung out like a giant arm to block the way of any hopeful traveller. These were the hills he'd seen from the chestnut tree.

It was about five miles between their cottage and the bit where the hills became mountains, where the contour lines suddenly grew much closer together, and Gareth had walked that way.

But where? *And what for?*

CHAPTER SIX

In the night the wardrobe door had swung open, revealing the beginnings of his hole. Robert examined the catch and saw that it was loose, so he got his screwdriver and tightened everything up. It'd be fatal if anyone came up here, glanced at the wardrobe and saw the mess he was making.

The debris from yesterday's session was still on the floor in a pile. He got it all on to a newspaper, opened the long drawer at the bottom of the wardrobe and tipped it inside. The drawer was deep and would hold quite a lot. As long as no-one came snooping he could do quite a few hours of useful excavation without the others being any the wiser.

The plaster on the 'false' wall was damp to the touch and it gave him an idea for an experiment. He crept across to the bathroom with his two oldest T-shirts folded into a thick pad and soaked them in cold water. Then he climbed into the wardrobe and squeezed it over the plaster. After a minute or so he tried levering a bit off with a chisel. It worked, and a big piece came away like a dream. Jubilantly, he opened the drawer and chucked it in.

He was rather pleased with himself. He would start on the pencilled circle section by section and get all the

47

plaster off, with the aid of wet T-shirts, then he could attack the wall itself. His fist told him it was depressingly solid though, anything but 'false', and if he allowed himself to think for very long about the whole project he was forced to admit that it was rather stupid. He didn't actually believe he'd find anything behind that wall, he was really making a hole in it because he was bored.

They were eating breakfast when something very noisy came clanking up the road and screeched to a halt outside the house as a dog started yapping. 'Stupid little bugger!' they heard, a man's voice, rather thin and nervous; then, '*Hush*, Idris.' This was somebody much more forceful, and female.

'It's the Preeces,' Dad said, going to the front door. 'Mr Preece said he'd come and help me shift that piano. Er, hello, Idris.'

But the dark little Welshman, somewhat overshadowed in size by his wife Dilys who was carefully unpacking herself from the sidecar of an old motor cycle, was still complaining about Rags who was now leaping up at him rapturously, his wet tongue hanging out. 'One of these days it'll get clobbered for good by something coming along this road,' he said, to nobody in particular, stamping at the dog to get it away from his trouser legs, and he shouted something very violent and threatening in Welsh, so loud that Rags whimpered and cowered away. It sounded like the most hideous swearing. '*Idris!*' Dilys said sharply, poking at him and pointing down at Nick who'd thrust his head through Dad's legs to see what was going on.

'Well, Morgan should have put it down last year, when the collie got its eye. It'd have been kinder. Wouldn't part with the money of course,' he added, looking at Dad. 'And it's limped for years, ugly little sod.'

'*Idris.*'

'I feel a bit sorry for it, actually,' Robert said.

'Oh aye, it's tough enough, and it's a real goer. You should see it when it gets in among Morgan's sheep though, it makes merry hell. I still say it'd be better out of its misery.'

'But it's the boy's dog, Idris, you know that. His dad keeps it because of the boy.' His wife freed herself at last from the sidecar and stepped out in to the lane, brushing the dust off.

Idris was little and squat, like a small pugnacious terrier. At his side, Dilys resembled a ship in full sail and she was definitely dressed up to go somewhere special. It surely couldn't be chapel, Robert decided, even though it was Sunday morning, not *chapel* in shocking pink, with that enormous hat and all that chunky jewellery. It glinted and gleamed in the morning sun as she stood there beaming at the three Elliott children. Mum and Ping had met her yesterday in Llandewi market but she'd looked quite different then, in her old green mac.

'That's a lovely family you've got, Mrs Elliott,' she said as Mum wandered out in her old dressing gown, to see who'd arrived; 'really beautiful.' Nick was staring open-mouthed at the enormous raven-haired lady in the bright pink suit and Robert was willing him not to say 'But why are you so fat?' It was the kind of thing he tended to say on buses. 'We're off to have dinner with Idris's brother in Holywell,' she went on, 'but we'll not be away long. Now, why don't you come down to my house this afternoon, the three of you, then your mam and dad can have a good rest, eh?'

49

And she bent down to chuck Nick under the chin. She loved children, she'd had five of her own. 'Come and see Mr Preece's rabbits,' she said. 'And we've got a swing in our garden. Now, Idris, what about that piano you've come to shift for Mr Elliott? We've not come for a little chat, is it?'

Robert watched as she steered Idris towards Aunt Em's junk-filled barn. Then he grinned at Ping. Dilys might liven things up a bit round here, she was so loud and theatrical-looking. He'd had another thought too, the Preeces just might know something about this cottage, they'd both been born and bred in the area. It was worth getting to know them.

Idris offered to show them all round the village while Dilys did tea but they couldn't get Ping away from the rabbits. Stupid animals, Robert thought privately, no brains at all. When you'd stroked their silky ears and wiggled a couple of lettuce leaves at them there was nothing left to do. They just munched away obliviously.

Nick hated walks and, anyway, they couldn't separate him from the swing. Whenever Robert lifted him down he grizzled. 'Leave him here, my darling,' Dilys called through the kitchen window. 'Unless he really wants to come. Do you want to go with Uncle Idris, my beauty?' To Robert's relief Nick shook his head vehemently and went on swinging and Ping, who was usually very women's lib about household chores, offered to set the table and butter bread in that irritating 'Christian' voice she'd recently developed. Robert was glad of the chance to go off with Idris on his own. He suspected that he might have a bit more to say for himself away from Dilys. He certainly had his views on Gareth's father, not to mention Rags whom he'd referred to several times as an 'ugly little bugger'.

The tiny village of Groeyurgoch was at the top of another steep hill and they toiled up it in silence, Idris sucking on a foul-smelling old pipe he'd lit up the minute they'd lost sight of Dilys. 'The wife's not too keen on me smoking,' he muttered and he puffed it furiously. 'She'll not have it in the house at all.'

It was his last utterance for a very long time and Robert soon realised that this walk with Idris wasn't going to be exactly productive. He was a man of very few words indeed, no doubt because he'd got used to his wife finishing all his sentences for him, and also because his pipe seemed to need constant love and attention, to prevent it going out. As they wandered round the grey huddled hamlet of Groeyurgoch, set deep in its small fields, he seemed quite happy to let Robert do the talking and he answered in grunts, or not at all.

The ancient graveyard behind the church was a major disappointment because all the stones were inscribed in Welsh. Robert had imagined that both Parrys and Morgans of the past might be buried in it and that he'd hear a bit more from Idris about the old family feud, but his questions got nil response. Idris only came to life on the subject of Reg Morgan who'd been in the paper that very week for taking some poor old man to court, over a land dispute. 'Mean bugger,' he said in a whisper, puffing ferociously.

'What's that, Idris?' Behind the church and across a barley field Robert had noticed something that looked like one of the tombstones in the graveyard, but it was a lot taller, and narrow towards the top, all on its own in the middle of a green-gold sea. 'That? Oh it's the

Parry Stone.' Idris didn't seem very interested. He relit his pipe and bent down to examine an ear of barley. 'This isn't doing too well,' he muttered, 'we could do with some better weather.'

'Can we have a look at it?'

Idris shrugged and opened the gate. 'If you want. It's not much, mind you.'

Robert followed him along the side of the field then across a short grassy swathe that led to the greening granite monument. When he got close to it he clicked his teeth in frustration: the writing was in Welsh again. 'Is it a grave?' he said.

'No, it's a historic monument, that's why they have to keep the grass cut short, for the tourists.'

'So – well, what happened here, then?'

Idris took a pair of glasses from his breast pocket and put them on. '*Near this spot*,' he read hesitantly, and with a thick Welsh accent, '*Emlyn Griffiths, farmer, found the Llandewi Treasure, 17th October 1920.* I remember Emlyn,' he said rather proudly, stepping back, 'he was a grand old man. Could do with a bit of a clean if you ask me.'

'And what was "the treasure"?'

'Oh not much, just a few bits and pieces, gold coins, jewellery. They all had the Parry mark on them, you know, that lion head. We were taken to see them as kids, from school, we went all the way to Bangor on a charabanc. Llandewi's got its own museum now though, and not before time if you ask me. This was local, this was. Emlyn turned it up with his plough. Didn't your mam go yesterday, when she was in town?'

'Yes, she did, and my sister bought some postcards of the jewellery. I didn't realise they'd dug it up *here*

52

though. I suppose,' he went on slowly, 'that there was border fighting all round here too, you know, between the main families?'

'Oh, I dare say. Bones still get turned up, now and again.' Idris laughed. 'They don't go running to the museum with them though, they just plough them back in. Too much fuss otherwise. Ready for home, then?'

Robert stared at him, and then at the Parry Stone, at the wind blowing through the barley, parting it like luxuriant green hair. And noises came to him, the clashing of swords and axes, the cries of human misery, horsemen clattering away towards the hills, their red cloaks streaming out behind them like bloody battle-flags. This peaceful ground had once been a field of blood. He felt it now.

Suddenly he took the plunge, looked straight at Idris and said, 'Someone told us there'd been a murder at our cottage once.' And the man's face suddenly changed. His pipe slipped sideways, fell from his mouth and disappeared in the grass. 'Who was that, then?' His voice was keener now, more guarded.

'Oh a person Aunt Em knew,' Robert said evasively. 'She mentioned it years ago, to Mum. I just wondered about it. I'm interested in things like that.'

'Well I'd not go bothering your head with creepy stories, lad, houses as old as your auntie's must have seen birth and death a hundred times, it's nature.'

'That's what my dad said.'

'Well, he's right. You listen to him and stop worrying your head,' and Idris pocketed his defunct pipe and set off briskly towards the gate.

But Robert followed very slowly, unconvinced.

53

He'd seen the pipe drop from Idris's mouth at the word 'murder'; and he'd not *denied* it.

'There's something the wife wanted me to warn you about,' Idris said as the Preeces' white-painted cottage came into view at the bottom of the hill, 'but don't go telling your little brother, mind. It's dangerous and the moors are littered with the things. It's a scandal, really. Those that own the land should fill them in. Here, keep to the wall.'

Robert followed him off the road again and into an overgrown tussocky field all broken up with boulders. Rabbits bounded away from Idris's boots as he picked his way across, making towards some decrepit white-painted posts fenced together with rusty barbed wire. 'Look at that,' he said pointing.

Robert followed his finger downwards, then recoiled. He was staring into a narrow circular hole about twenty feet deep. At the bottom was the decayed carcass of a sheep, its head picked clean down to the skull and its mouth wide open in a hideous grin.

'Yuk!' he said, stepping back. The smell from the shaft was indescribable.

'Not a pretty sight, is it?' Idris said evenly. 'It's an old mine shaft, in case you're wondering. They found coal round here in the old days, not much mind you, it's in South Wales mainly, coal is. Yes, there are old workings all over this place and they're bloody dangerous, I can tell you. This field's Reg Morgan's.' He'd got his pipe out again and was spitting into the grass. 'If anyone had an accident down one of these he'd be ruined, that man would. Serve him damned well right too.'

'Er, are there many shafts, Idris?' Instead of the

54

grinning sheep at the bottom of the hole Robert saw Nick, with his neck broken.

'There's enough. Listen, if you ever see a big round patch, where the grass looks a bit spongy like, keep away. It'll be a shaft. They put rubble down them but sometimes the earth caves in again, especially in very wet weather. You keep away from places like that, the other two as well. That's my advice any road.'

'We will.' He wasn't even going to mention what Idris had shown him. His kid brother, with his passion for going to the very edge of station platforms and wanting to jump off the top diving board at Buckden Baths (when he couldn't even swim) would adore the idea of an old discarded mineshaft to play in.

Dilys was standing at the cottage gate with Nick leaning over it, looking up the road. 'Yoo hoo!' he yelled, 'you two!' Idris shoved his pipe hastily into his pocket and pulled at his shirt collar, seeming instinctively to quicken his pace.

Robert speeded up too. He was going to make the most of Dilys's special tea. Now Mum was hooked on Welsh history and playing Aunt Em's piano, there was no telling where the next good meal would come from.

CHAPTER SEVEN

He'd got a bag of home-baked goodies in his rucksack and he thought of Dilys rather guiltily as he put his thumbs through the straps and strode out across the moor. She was down at Aunt Em's cleaning round now the extra furniture was installed. He'd watched rather nervously as she'd produced dusters, brooms and buckets from the understairs cupboard, hoping against hope that her mini spring cleaning session wouldn't include dusting behind the wardrobes.

He felt guilty all round, because he'd misled just about everybody. Dilys had packed him a picnic for one of the 'long solitary walks' he'd described so convincingly, and Mum and Dad had let him cry off their trip to the seaside because he'd complained of vague 'headaches and sore throat'. *They'd* imagined he'd spend today quietly indoors, at Aunt Em's. Nobody really knew what his plan was, trailing Gareth Morgan and, this time, not letting him go.

It had rained for two solid days since Dilys's tea-party and the general boredom had reached crisis point. Ping was OK because she was a bookworm; she'd made herself a nest in a corner of the big settee, next to the fire, and spent endless hours reading. She'd also spent hours writing a long letter to Sally.

Nick had been a pain in the neck, though. He'd whinged on and on about no TV, and nobody to play with, and nowhere to ride his bike which they hadn't been able to bring anyway. Dad had finally lost his temper and gone off into one of his rages. He'd been trying to work at the kitchen table and Nick had spilt a whole bottle of black ink over one of Steeles' precious plans.

Mum hadn't exactly helped by promising Nick a trip to the coast the minute the weather cleared up, which had made him ten times worse. Every other second it was 'Has it stopped raining yet?' and 'When can we *go*?' Robert had crept up to his bedroom to avoid Dad's wrath, and had another quiet plaster-picking session in his wardrobe.

Mum's idea of a packed lunch was minimal – a packet of biscuits, an apple and crisps if you were lucky, but Dilys obviously had the siege mentality, he'd decided, as he watched her cutting sandwiches.

'That's OK, really,' he protested as she embarked on a fourth round of cheese and pickle, 'I can't eat all that.' He could, but he didn't want too much to carry, he might have to follow Gareth for miles if he did go off on another of those mysterious 'errands' towards the hills, and Robert's hunch was that he would, just as soon as the weather dried up.

He was right, too: he'd spotted him going off up the fields not ten minutes after their car had driven off down the lane, and he'd set off after him. From Morgan's hilltop farm you could spy quite nicely on the comings and goings at Aunt Em's. Gareth must have waited till the Elliotts were out of the way before setting off himself. He wasn't to know that one of them had stayed behind.

Robert had always imagined that country people didn't talk much but Dilys was quite a gossip, and he'd led her on shamelessly. Rags wasn't with Gareth this time, he noticed, and she'd told him why. The dog was chained up at the farm in disgrace because he'd been running amok with the sheep again. Morgan had threatened to destroy Rags if Gareth didn't control him better. 'And it's a shame,' she said fiercely, slapping butter thickly on currant bread, 'the boy doesn't have much to call his own, and he loves that poor dog. And there's that scholarship he got too, a crying shame that was. He's doing a piece at the Llandewi Eisteddfod this summer and I don't suppose his da will come to that, either. He told my Idris there was no money in music, just in muck. Oh, that *man*, darling . . .' and she slapped the buttered slices together venomously, as if Morgan's bullet head was trapped between them.

It seemed that Gareth had once been offered a place at the famous Cathedral Choir School in Llandewi but that his father had turned it down flat, even though Mr Jenkins had come up from the village primary, and Miss Powell his piano teacher, to plead with him. 'It would have meant him leaving home, my darling,' she'd explained, 'and his dad didn't want that. He doesn't want the boy out of his sight yet he treats him like dirt. There you are. That enough for you, is it?'

'Just about,' he said, stowing it all in the rucksack. 'It'll last me till lunch-time, anyhow. Thanks very much.'

He was walking steadily, letting Gareth get as far ahead as possible but speeding up if he threatened to disappear from sight, like last time. They were both wearing bright red sweaters and Gareth showed up garishly against the dun-coloured moorland. They were on a definite path, a kind of causeway, drier than the land on each side. When he slipped off it his shoe disappeared into mud, the colour and consistency of molasses.

He lost a few minutes at one point, looking at a patch of sunken earth just off the track. It was a rough circle covered with small boulders that gleamed up through the grass. Here, too, a hopeful farmer must have dug for coal, years ago. He remembered the grinning sheep and Idris's bleak warning, and thought of Nick on a chilly beach, sand in the sandwiches and hopeless baby cricket. He shouldn't really have left Ping to cope with him on her own but this secret walk of his might just lead to something and, if it did, deceiving them all wouldn't matter so much, he reasoned, as he tramped along.

He followed Gareth for a good hour through land that became increasingly more barren and desolate. It was boggy and wet, miles from a road, not even picturesque. Nobody would come here without a very good reason. He was getting tired, too, and he thought about stopping for a minute, to get something to eat out of the rucksack. But as he slowed his pace he saw the red blob of Gareth's sweater moving up to a line of thick trees that bristled up out of the bluey landscape, like green spines on a porcupine's back. He felt a little stab of excitement and quickened up again. Perhaps they were really getting somewhere at last.

When he reached the wood he saw that it wasn't a deep forest going back and back but a mere belt of tangled cover for the rocks that reared up above his head. He'd come to a solid stone face overgrown with creepers. Through the green, rock gleamed white, like an animal's teeth bared to do battle.

Gareth had disappeared. Robert stared at the rock in disbelief because he could see no way of getting up it, and yet the path had definitely ended. Then, at ground level, he suddenly noticed brown where it should have been green. A heap of dead branches at his feet had been bunched together by somebody, as if to make a bonfire.

He peered into the brown criss-cross then realised it was black behind the branches, not white. He pulled the rotting wood apart and in a couple of minutes had exposed a crack in the rock wall. A fissure, roughly tent-shaped, about four feet across at the bottom and tapering up to nothing, yawned out at him. He took off his rucksack and felt in one of the pouches for the pencil torch he always kept there, dumped the rucksack under a bush and clicked the switch. Then he climbed into the hole.

At first there was a faint green light round him but soon the crack turned into a real tunnel. For a minute Robert looked back. He could see a thicket with its fresh green branches waving in the wind, he could hear the birds. Then he went forwards into total darkness.

The passage was so narrow he had to inch along sideways to avoid getting stuck. The tunnel roof brushed at his hair as he thrust his head down between his shoulders like a predatory bird. Then the weak torchlight flickered and died.

He stopped and leaned against the rock wall and the silence throbbed around him. Deep in his stomach a worm of panic had started to wriggle and gnaw. He feld giddy and sick and it was as though the tunnel had started to close in on him, as if the ceiling was sagging down. Somewhere, far away, he thought he heard a faint scattering of pebbles. A rock fall was beginning. He would be entombed.

A cry came to his lips but he swallowed it back. Was this the end of everything, to be lost in the stone heart of a bleak Welsh hillside? Nobody would find him because nobody knew where he was. He would have given anything, at that moment, to have Nick's sticky little paw buried trustingly in his own.

But he stumbled on blindly, fighting the tears back. Then he trod on something that crackled and he groped round by his feet. His fingers closed on a small object that smelt minty when he held it to his face. Gradually, as he stood there shaking, it turned into a striped humbug squashed flat by someone's heel.

He could see the sweet so there must be light somewhere. The tunnel was turning into a crack again and he could see trees. But to get through he had to wriggle underneath a huge arm of rock that almost blocked the path. Only someone of his size, or smaller, could have got through.

At last he could straighten up and he looked all round for Gareth. Ahead of him, leading away from the tunnel, was a narrow stony track that plunged almost instantly into thick trees. He laboured up it, hearing a rush of water somewhere above him, a sound that got steadily louder as he gained height. Then the track ended abruptly and he had to pull up smartly to avoid falling several hundred feet down, on to sharp rocks.

He was standing on the rim of a kind of canyon with steep rocky sides. Just below him a stream gushed out

61

of the hill and emptied itself in a single great sweep into a small lake, far below. The canyon was a rough oval, not much more than half a mile from end to end. Straight across, on the opposite edge, was more woodland. Trees ringed the entire valley blotting out any views and softening into leafiness what must be a much harsher landscape in winter.

The valley floor was quite flat and green and he could see a cow and a couple of sheep. At one end there was a lot of rubble and several crumbling walls smothered in bracken fronds. It looked like the grown-over remains of quite a large house. At the other end, near the waterfall, he could see an old hut with a decrepit shed built behind it, up a slope. One side had blaring white letters daubed all over it but he was too far off to make out what they said.

He edged forwards cautiously over slithery rocks looking for a safe way down and spotted a rocky zig-zag path hurtling into the valley, by the side of the waterfall. He started to pick his way along it, stopping now and then to look at the hut, to see if he could decipher the white painted message, but he was still too far away. All was quiet. The animals down below munched on placidly and smoke curled up from the hut chimney into the flat sky.

Then he saw Gareth come out from behind the rickety shed and there was a clanging noise as an old oil drum toppled and rolled bouncing down one of the rocks, in front of the hut. The boy started to run, skirting the lake then glancing up at the canyon wall where Robert stood spread-eagled by the waterfall like a red X, staring down at him. A man came out of the hut and started to wave his arms about, shouting loudly in Welsh and staring up the valley.

Gareth was climbing rapidly up the rocky path. His face was sweaty and red, his eyes bulged and he gobbled at the air for breath. When he got level he pushed Robert to one side and went on climbing, not once looking back.

The hard shove was enough to make him lose his balance. His rubber soles slithered off the rock and he started to bump crazily down the valley side, heading straight for the great waterfall. He screamed and shut his eyes, clutching out wildly to save himself.

But there was no need. A second or two later his flight was ended by arms that grabbed him and held him rigidly, like steel pincers, and he was hustled down the track towards the hut. Then he was flung into the shed behind it and a heavy wooden door was slammed to and bolted, leaving him in darkness.

CHAPTER EIGHT

At first he was as blind in the shed as he had been in the rocky tunnel, but gradually his eyes adjusted to the dark and he could see light seeping through in several places. The door was full of knot holes and the sunshine filtered through them, riddling the earth floor with speckles of light.

He crept over to it, peering through one of the holes. The man who'd locked him in was leaning over a water-butt on the corner of the hut. Robert could hear him swishing his hands round, then footsteps going back to the hut and another door slamming. Through the hole he could see that the bit of wall behind the wooden tub was daubed like the side of the shed and he was close enough now to read what it said. 'Rats Are Vermin' the crude white capitals told him and the paint had made big splashes down the side of the water butt.

The man had obviously mistaken him for Gareth who'd got up the valley path too quickly for him to realise that there were two of them. They were about the same age though Robert was taller and skinnier; from a distance, though, nobody would spot that. They'd both been wearing red sweaters. Gareth's was the reindeer one; he didn't seem to have any others.

Robert shifted his position slightly, to get a better view of the outside. But the hut door had opened again and the knot-hole suddenly turned black. Someone came in and took him roughly under the armpits, propelling him outside, then he was pushed along towards the hut, the man kicking him from behind to hurry him up. Once inside, he was forced on to a chair. He was in a dark stuffy room that stank of animals and an old man in a corner was staring at him. Most of the space was taken up with a rough table and on it were three dead rats.

The man who'd locked him in picked up one of the bodies by the tail and thrust it under Robert's nose, shouting angrily. Water dripped from it and wet his face. The smell was unbearable and his stomach lurched violently. He turned his face away and shook his head. 'I'm not the boy you're looking for,' he said, 'so you can just leave me alone and let me go. It's Gareth Morgan you want and he got away, through that crack in the rocks.'

The man threw the rat back on to the table and came right up to him, staring hard, then he looked at the old man who was nodding and muttering to himself. The younger one kept prodding at Robert's sweater but the old one was pointing at his hair. It was a wild blond thatch that stuck out like straw, whereas Gareth's was dark and greasy.

They started to quarrel then, the son pacing up and down by the table, jabbing at the rats while he poured out a flood of angry Welsh, still pointing at Robert, and glowering. He had a thick dark beard and longish hair, uncombed and all matted together, and his ancient suit had safety pins holding the trousers together. The old man sat huddled with a sack round his shoulders.

His grizzled beard looked as if it must once have been red. The right side of his mouth was all pulled down and his right hand sat uselessly in his lap. He'd obviously had a stroke, like Grandad Elliott before he died. Eventually he lapsed into silence but the other man was still banging on the table, and yelling. Then he thrust his fist right under Robert's chin.

OK, that was it. The boy got up and made for the door. After all, it hadn't been locked behind them and there was nothing to prevent his walking straight through it. The man grabbed him and tried to force him back on to the chair but Robert shook him off and stared at the two of them, across the room. Somehow he didn't feel so scared of them any more; he sensed that they were more frightened than he was.

'Just let me go, will you,' he told them. 'I'm not responsible for these, if that's what you're thinking,' and he pointed at the rats. The man's hand had dislodged one and its head was lolling over the end of the table, its teeth bared.

Now he knew. There must have been a rat in Gareth's rucksack, the day he'd lost him when he was up in the chestnut tree spying. He remembered now that Rags had been going crazy to get inside it. Was that why he'd had the gun then? What did you need to shoot rats with?

Suddenly the man slumped down into a chair and faced Robert across the table. At last he seemed to have got the message about the mix up between the two boys. 'What are you doing here then? Why did you come with the other one? And how did you know what he'd been doing to us?' His English was slow and very heavily accented, as if he didn't speak the language very often and had to think carefully about it.

'I *didn't* know,' Robert said. 'I was just suspicious of him, that's all. We'd tried to make friends with him but he was horrible to us and before that I'd found him up our field with a pistol. He'd fired it at me as well, he was obviously trying to scare me off. I knew he must be up to something because he kept going off through the fields and disappearing. So today I followed him, just to see.'

'And what was it like, this gun?'

'It was an air pistol, I think, I don't really know. He said he'd only shot *past* me, but that was a lie. He was aiming at me all right.'

'Guns, always guns,' the old man mumbled and his awful lopsided mouth dribbled as he spoke. 'They love guns, the Morgans do.'

'Oh be quiet, Dad.' The younger man sounded embarrassed. 'My father lives in the past these days,' he told Robert, and the voice was gentler now.

'We've had a quiet time of it in the last few years, nobody's bothered us at all. Then, last spring, that boy kept coming, and things started up again.'

'What things?'

'Morgan. I'm sure he's behind it. Keeps sending his boy here through the crack in the rocks, it's like a game he's playing. Every time he comes it's something different.

'The first time he just stood at the valley head and stared at us, then he came with a gun. The third time he started a fire then he – look, I'll show you. Come out here.'

He took Robert outside with him and pointed to the white letters on the side of the hut. 'He did that.' Then he showed him the writing on the shed.

'Filthy rats – rats stink' it said. 'Today there were rats

in the water-butt. Last week, when I got back from Llandewi, there was one in the bread crock. He's a filthy little pig, that boy is. He thinks because we live out here we don't know how to conduct ourselves. It's him needs showing, him and his father, not us.'

The dead rats had made Robert feel extremely queasy. In silence he followed the man back into the hut and sat down on a stool.

'D'you want a drink of water? You've lost all your colour. Here, come on, have a drink. It's all right – this is spring water, this is.' A cup was got down from an old dresser, and a jug brought out from a back room.

'No thanks, I just feel a bit sick. I'll be OK in a minute.' Then he said suddenly, 'But can you tell me something? Why's Reg Morgan doing this to you? And who are you, anyhow?'

There was an awful silence and the man glared at him balefully. In his corner the old man dribbled and shook, a single tear coursing slowly down his cheek.

Then the son said, 'Our family's always owned this valley. This land's ours, in spite of Reg Morgan and his solicitors' letters. That ruin outside, that was a big house once, our summer house, for when the sheep were in the out pastures. We still pay our way. We're not thieves and we're not tinkers either.'

'I'm very sorry, I didn't mean . . .' Robert stammered nervously, but the man was getting too agitated to listen properly. '*That one*,' he shouted, '*he's* the thief! *He's* the liar! Now his son's started lying too. Oh, Reg Morgan's very rich now, very grand, from all I hear. So he gets that son of his to do his dirty work for him. He's mad, I'm telling you.'

'So why does Morgan send you letters, then?'

'Because he says the valley's his, and he want us out of it. He's threatened to take us to court about it now. That'll cost him. It's been in all the newspapers.'

'But what use could land out here be to him? This place is miles from anywhere, and there's no road. Well, not that I could see.'

'Oh yes, there's a road,' the man told him. 'A track goes down to it, from here. You could improve it, put tarmac on and that. It's what he's planning to do. Money's no object to him, not when he's got big plans.'

'But this isn't farming land, surely?'

'Oh, Morgan doesn't want to farm it, he wants to sell it off to Peele. But he can't, because it's ours.'

'That's right, son, it's ours. Peele can't get his hands on our land, son.' The single tear on the old man's cheek had been joined by others now. He was whimpering childishly in his chair and still drooling from the corner of his mouth. The son went over to him and dabbed gently at his face. 'It's all right,' Robert heard him whisper, 'this boy's not from Morgan. That boy's gone. It's all right, Dad.'

'Who's Peele?' It was terrible to see the old man weeping. The inert right arm and the crooked mouth reminded him of his grandfather. He couldn't bear to look at him so he looked at the dirty matting that covered the floor instead.

'Oliver Peele,' the son said, 'the carpet millionaire. Peele's Discount Carpets. Haven't you heard of them?'

'Yes, yes I have. There's one of their shops where we live. But that's not Welsh is it, *Peele*?'

'No, but his family was from round here, way back. Came up from nothing, that lot did. Peele's always fancied this valley. He's got a big estate outside Chester but he wants to build a holiday house here. Morgan says he'll sell it to him, too.'

'But it's yours, you've just said so.'

'Of course it is, but we can't prove it, can we? We've no money for solicitors and that's how he'll catch us in the end. We've always lived in this valley and everybody round here knows that. It won't stop him, though.'

'We've always been here,' his father repeated dully, reaching out towards the table with agonising slowness and trying to pull Robert's untouched cup of water towards him.

'Here, Dad.' Very carefully the man brought it up to his lips and helped him drink. Robert watched in silence. Inside he wanted to cry. What was such a sick old man doing in a place like this with the son having to do everything for him? And why did they cling to it so? Animals lived better than they did. But he didn't dare say anything, or ask too many questions. There was a pride about these people.

'Morgan's always wanted this place.' The man set the cup down on the table, wiped his father's mouth and eased him more comfortably in his chair. 'Years ago he used to come through the rocks himself, spying on us and that. It's ten miles round by the road. But he got too fat for it in the end, it was the drink that was. He drinks every night now, from what I hear. It started when the wife died.'

The old man was still crying. Suddenly, he reached up with his good hand and clutched at the son's fingers. Robert, still staring at the floor, wondered about them. Why hadn't the son got married himself and taken his father away from the valley? What would happen if the old man suddenly got much worse, or had another stroke, and nobody would come? There was no sign of a telephone and in winter the snow would surely cut the place off completely. There was so much he wanted to know yet they'd think his questions were idle curiosity, prying even.

'Was that your house?' he said at last. 'The big one, out there by the waterfall? Did you used to live in that?' He thought they'd be pleased, perhaps, if he associated them with a grand house. For all the stink and squalor in this miserable hut there was something about these two men. He couldn't exactly say what it was, except that the son looked like the father and that their keen, fine features, under the dirt, reminded him of saints' faces, chiselled from stone in some great cathedral.

As Robert spoke the son glanced through the open door. 'Ne'er,' he replied rather scornfully, 'we've never lived there, that was just a summer house, to live in when the sheep were brought up from the lower valleys. The family was rich then, richer than the Morgans ever were. Morgans couldn't hold a candle to us then.'

'But he wants the land,' the old man repeated yet again. He was calmer now and his good hand had dropped back into his lap. 'Land's power, son. He'd want it even without the Peele money. Power, that's what the Morgans have always wanted. I detest them,' and he spat on the floor.

After a minute the son said gruffly 'So . . . where do you come from, then?'

'Buckden Heath.'

'And where's that?'

'Just a bit south of Manchester. It's an awful place.'

'What do you mean, "awful"?'

For the first time Robert felt something other than open hostility. Both men were looking at him, wanting to hear more. They probably didn't see outsiders, from one week's end to the next. Strangers were big news in this valley.

'Well it's a town, for a start, and I don't like towns. It's filthy too, you know, all factories. I like the cottage better. I wish we could live here instead, but there's no work for Dad.'

'Which cottage?'

'It's near Groeyurgoch, up on the hill. Do you know the one I mean?'

The minute he'd said it he realised it was a stupid question. He'd not seen a single dwelling between Aunt Em's and this valley, but there'd been a definite track between one and the other. And these men would know every tree round here, every blade of grass.

'Aye, we know it. The Castell.'

'I've not heard it called that. We don't call it anything.'

'Castell's it's name. Weekending are you?' The old man's wavering voice had soured. 'Renting it for little holidays?'

'*No*. It belongs to Aunt Em, that's my mother's aunt. She's selling it when she comes back from New Zealand. We're just, you know, well – caretaking. She thought it'd be nice for us.'

'Own it, does she? Are you quite sure of that?' The old man was trying to push himself up out of his chair and his voice was threatening. The easier atmosphere in the dark fetid room had hardened again; it felt worse than before.

'Come on, Dad, the boy's all right,' the son said rather wearily, but his father had started to shake and he was making a weird moaning noise. Robert backed away, glancing towards the open door and the wind-blown grass beyond it. He could make his escape easily now, there was no need to stay here and be attacked, just for being English. These people were no better than Gareth Morgan.

'I said are you sure this auntie owns it, this . . . your mam's auntie?'

' 'Course I'm sure.'

'Well you're wrong, boyo. I know who owns the Castell at Groeyurgoch and all its lands.'

'Well, *who*?'

'I do, *me*,' and the one good hand rapped on the withered chest.

'*Dad*. Take no notice,' the son muttered to Robert. 'He's wandering now, he's going back years. It'll be all right in a minute.'

'And what's your name then, you people at the Castell?'

'Elliott. I'm Robert, Robert William Elliott.' The 'William' was after lovely Granddad, who'd had the stroke.

The old man's face softened slightly and he pulled at his chin, turning the name over in his mind, like wine in his mouth. 'I like that, it's a good name you've got. There's history in that.'

'What's yours, then?'

There was a prolonged silence. Perhaps, Robert was thinking, they just wouldn't tell. In fairy stories, when you gave a man your name, you gave him power over you, and this old man had talked a lot about power. But at last the voice came out of the chimney corner, quite firm and ringing out in the quietness. 'We're from kings,' it said, 'the kings of Wales.'

'Oh Dad, for heavens *sake*.' The son exchanged embarrassed looks with Robert and lifted up his hands rather helplessly.

'How do you know, though?' It was the question Nick had asked Mum, in the car. 'How can anyone really know a thing like that? I mean we could all –'

'We *know*,' the old voice interrupted. 'I've told you, we've always been here. See?'

'Get my box down,' he ordered his son suddenly.

'Dad, why don't you just go and have a lie down?'

'I said, *fetch* it. Want proof, do you? All right.'

Robert watched as the son climbed up on to the table and rooted about on a shelf. After a minute he got down again and set a rusty tin box in front of the old man. He even opened it for him and took bundles of papers out. It was obviously a well-worn ritual.

'You interested in old coins?' The father was shaking a little bag out on to the table. The contents looked like Pontefract cakes, very thick and black, and there were some war medals too, on dirty ribbons.

'Yes, I am, as a matter of fact. I've got a collection at home.' Well, he used to have, till Nick got at it. A lot of his coins were missing now, thanks to Nick and his little friend Craig. 'Where did you get these?'

'Dug them up, didn't I, years ago, when I was building the shed. Worth money, these are. I bet Morgan'd like to get his hands on this lot.'

Then Robert saw the ring. The rats were still lying on the table but he plucked up all his courage, stretched past them and took it in his hand. It was enormous, crudely hammered and very thick, faintly scored with the markings of a lion head.

'Watch what you're doing with that,' the old man said sharply. 'It's gold, that is.'

'I know.' It was like the one on Ping's postcards from the Old Fire Station Museum. The two looked identical. 'Did you dig this up, too?' he asked.

'*Ne'er*, give it here.' And he put it back in the bag. 'We've always had that. It's really old that is, it's a proper antique. My father gave it to me and his father gave it to him. It's been in our family for hundreds of years, that has,' the old man said proudly.

There was a sudden burst of sun outside. The light came through a little window behind the sagging chair, shining down on the old man's head, and Robert could see his face properly for the first time. He was small, and shrunk even smaller by old age; yet he looked noble. Thick white hair sprang strongly back from a broad jutting forehead, he had a long straight nose and a deeply-clefted chin, and the sun that poured down on him through the narrow glass seemed to make the pale weak eyes burn again.

Kings were the men who'd proved themselves, Mum had told Nick in Church Stoken, the strongest ones, the noblest. Just for a second Robert felt he was looking, not at a sick, frightened old man but at a great leader.

He said 'You've still not told me your names,' but he knew now.

'We've got the same name, me and my son here, it's Daniel, Daniel Parry. Everyone calls him Dan but I'm Daniel, always have been. My mam wanted that. Aye, it's a good old name.'

Robert did a double-take when he looked down at his watch. It was hours later than he thought, he'd got to get back. But when he was going out of the door the

75

old man, who'd levered himself out of the chair and shuffled painfully across the floor, dragging his leg, gripped his arm fiercely. 'Listen,' he said. 'You tell that Morgan boy to leave off coming here. Two can play at his game. We've got guns too. You tell him that.' It was true. Robert had seen a shotgun in a corner when he first came in.

'But I've told you what he's like,' he said. 'It's no good me talking to him, he won't listen. He hates our family. He fired a pistol at me the very first time I saw him. I told you that. You ought to get a solicitor on to him, or the police. Yes, why don't you go to the police?' But old Daniel Parry didn't seem to hear. His eyes had filled up again and he wouldn't let go of Robert's arm. 'You tell him,' he repeated. 'He might listen to you. Tell him we've got guns.'

The boy looked down into his face and his heart went out to him. He didn't look like a great chieftain any more, just a dirty, terrified old man. Perhaps they had their own private reasons for not calling the police in, and solicitors cost money which they obviously didn't have.

He said 'I'll speak to him, I promise I will, and I'll tell him he'll be in big trouble if he does anything else. I really will have a go.' And he pressed the good hand that was still hooked on to his arm. 'Only I've got to get home now or I'll be in trouble myself. They don't know where I am.' He wasn't going to admit it but he was scared of going back through that tunnel, and to do the journey across the moors in darkness was unthinkable. The sooner he was off the better now.

He didn't say anything else but he watched in silence as Dan hunted for a flashlight for him to take through the rocks, and pulled old boots on. 'I'll come with you to the valley head,' he said, knotting the laces and standing up.

'OK, but can we go now? It'll take me hours to get home.'

Dan took him on a track that went straight up by the waterfall, not the grassy zig-zag where he'd collided with Gareth. It was horribly steep and they climbed it without stopping once. He was sweaty and panting when he reached the top and a sharp pain was cutting across his chest. Dan had gone up springily, like a mountain goat.

'You all right?' he said as they stood at the head of the waterfall. Robert nodded in reply, he didn't have the breath to speak. Instead, he stared down at the great rush of water, watching it foam and spray over the huge rocks below. The path was green and slippery just here and he edged back. You could break your neck if you once lost your footing, and fell.

'Ta ra then.' Rather awkwardly Dan handed him the rubber torch. 'You can hang on to this for now, I've got another.' Then he put his hand on Robert's sleeve. 'I'm sorry about my dad, going on at you and that, but it's the Morgan boy. He can't stand much more of it, it's going to bring on another stroke. You tell him what we've said, will you? One more visit from him, playing his daft tricks, and – well, he'd better watch it, that's all. We've had enough.'

'I'll tell him.' Robert couldn't think what good it would do, but he'd decided he was going to anyway even before he'd promised the old man. Gareth Morgan couldn't know how sick he was, or how frightened. If he did know, then he was being cruel.

Dan's torch made the tunnel much less scary and he squeezed through very quickly, before he could think about it. Then he set off rapidly across the moors towards Aunt Em's, too fast, he realised, when another violent stitch forced him to slow down. But he was panicking. He wanted to get back before the others came home from the sea. Dilys would have packed up and gone long ago, so there'd be no awkward questions from her; but Dad might ask a few. As he walked, he thought hard about the Parrys in their desolate valley, and about Ping's scrapbook and that ring. He'd like to do the impossible, borrow it and take it to the experts in the Old Fire Station Museum. The two rings were the same, he knew they were. But he couldn't see the old man parting with it, not even for a few days.

He tried to remember what Mum had told them about the Parry-Morgan feud. They'd both been really great families once, then wealthy farmers, and Morgan was still wealthy, according to what everyone said, even though he lived in such a mean way. He was supposed to own thousands of acres and three or four other farms. But the Parrys had ended up in that remote canyon miles from anywhere. They'd abandoned the good rich land round Aunt Em's, even though it had all been theirs, all the land from the cottage to the valley.

What had happened to them? Why was nothing left of all that wealth and power but an old man and his son, scrabbling to survive in a kind of tip, in a house no better than a pig-sty? Something horrific and unspeakable must have driven them into that narrow valley, something bloody and terrible that nobody ever spoke about, something the Parrys had never recovered from. Gareth Morgan had told him of a murder in their own cottage. Was it a lie or did he really know something?

And Robert had seen the ring. That, he felt sure, was the key to it all. They couldn't possibly know about the other one, displayed on red velvet in the museum, the 9th century ring of 'Daniel the Great Leader'. The old man was much too proud of his relics not to have told him a thing like that. It was the open, simple way he'd told him who he was that convinced Robert.

He climbed over the familiar fence at last, into Aunt Em's top field, saw the little white cottage down below, and started to run down, his heart thumping with a strange excitement.

He had found the tiny pathetic remnant of the great Parry tribe, the lion family, the Parrys of Clwyd. It was true.

CHAPTER NINE

That night Robert couldn't sleep because of night-mares about the men in the valley. They'd both come to dinner dressed like battle warriors out of a story book and Mum was serving them soup from a huge tureen. When it was his turn she lifted the lid off and he saw a decomposed rat floating in it. Dad was saying irritably, 'Hurry up, will you, I've not had any yet.'

He'd got back to the cottage only ten minutes before they had. There'd just been time to put a match to the fire Dilys had laid in the big room, and settle himself on the settee with a book trying to look as if he'd been there all day.

But Dad's irritation in the dream was real enough at breakfast next morning and Robert was glad to get out of the house, though the last thing he felt like doing was going to talk to Gareth Morgan. While he was getting dressed he'd heard his parents arguing. It sounded as if Mum wasn't feeling well though she was protesting to Dad that she was perfectly all right, and telling him not to fuss. He said she was 'overtired' and that the doctor should look at her. Remember what had happened when she'd had Nick, he'd reminded her.

Robert could remember Nick's birth perfectly

because Mum had been in hospital for several weeks before it happened, and he'd really hated it. Her blood pressure had shot up so they'd taken her into the Borough General in Buckden, to rest in bed until the baby arrived, hoping it wouldn't come too early and be too small, too feeble to survive.

That was the first time he'd ever been parted from his mother for more than a few hours and he could still remember the awful empty feeling of the quiet tidy house. Grandma Elliott had looked after meals and clothes a thousand times better than Mum yet he'd missed her agonisingly, pining for her every single night under his clean bedclothes, in his clean ironed pyjamas with all the buttons sewn back on.

All through that time he'd never once felt warm and now, nearly six years later, he still felt cold if he got home from school, shouted through to the back to 'check in' with Mum and found she wasn't there.

Dad had gone all silent on them when Mum was in hospital waiting for Nick and he'd hated that too, it had been worse than his rages. This time, thank goodness, it sounded as though he was fussing about nothing. Even so, Robert listened very carefully through his open door, as he laced up his sneakers.

'I'm perfectly all right,' Mum was saying calmly. 'I just said I felt a bit tired, after yesterday, that's all. I've got an appointment at the clinic next Tuesday, anyway. Now stop fussing, Jack. We can stay till the end of the week. Don't let's spoil the holiday.'

'All right, all *right*!' and their door had been slammed so he'd not heard anything else. He didn't like the shouting. His parents didn't argue very often, so when they did it was an Event. He wondered if his mother really was all right and whether Dad was just fussing.

81

The farm was deserted when he arrived. Morgan's battered estate car was parked in the yard and he could see cardboard boxes full of shopping in the back. Robert peeped into the kitchen. The dingy room looked just the same, piles of newspapers everywhere, the stained dark red arm-chairs huddled round the range. He could hear music coming from a radio and then Gareth's gran shuffled in, humming along with it in an old cracked voice. She looked happy.

'Hello,' he said, stepping inside. 'Do you know where Gareth is?'

When she saw who it was she beamed, and came to the door, then looked quickly behind him. Perhaps she was hoping he'd brought the others. Or was she on the look-out for Morgan? She started getting cups down from a shelf.

'I can't stay. I'm looking for Gareth. D'you know where he is?' he repeated.

She put the cups down and joined her knobbly hands together, composing herself for what was obviously going to be a mighty effort. He'd not heard her speak English, and Gareth had said she couldn't. But she said, very slowly and clearly, 'He's at his Auntie Margaret's in Llandewi, with his cousins. They're bringing him back later. He went down early this morning, to do the big shopping, with his father.'

At that moment Rags bounded in. He went straight to the range and shook himself over the rug, then he leaped up at Robert, yapping and licking his face. The boy patted him. He was so ugly, and pathetic with his chopped-off tail, his dead eye and his awful limp. But Robert had never known such a friendly, forgiving creature. Nobody bothered with him much, he was always getting shouted at, and kicked out of the way, but he went on loving. He wouldn't have minded a dog like that himself. Dogs were superior to most people, he'd decided.

Gareth's gran shooed him out and he went off to sit under the estate car. Robert could see his one brown eye peering out hopefully.

'I'll go back, then,' he said. 'I might come again later.' As he went towards the gate the old lady ran after him and shoved something into his hand, looking round again nervously before disappearing into the kitchen. Inside the bread-paper wrapping was a slice of *barabrith*, the wonderful speckled bread, dark with currants and thickly buttered. Good old Gran. He munched it greedily as he set off down the track.

As he walked he heard barking somewhere, far off, up to his right. It couldn't be Rags, he'd left him humped up mournfully in the yard, no doubt waiting for Gareth to come back. Then he heard the confused bleating of what must be dozens of sheep, then a man's harsh commands. He climbed over a gate into a field and started to follow the path along a hedge.

The noises got louder. He'd almost crossed the top of the field and reached a fence. Beyond was a huge meadow. It swept away down the curve of the land like a vast green quilt, and in the middle a flock of sheep was moving as one.

Morgan was standing in the field with his back to Robert, yelling orders to Beth, the black and white collie. His cries were neither English nor Welsh but a strange half-sung, half-spoken kind of language that only the dog understood. According to Dilys, it was being trained up for the North Wales Sheepdog Trials in the autumn. The man had obviously taken a few hours off to put it through its paces.

Robert stood in the shadow of a hedge, half-hidden. He didn't want to be accused of trespassing. Beth drove the sheep down to the bottom of the meadow and forced them through a gateway. There were six left on Morgan's side and Robert could see him making a kind of enclosure with oil drums and old pieces of fencing.

Then he called to her and she bounded up the field, zig-zagging across the grass in short runs, driving the six sheep down towards the fold. One kept wandering off to nibble at something under the hedge. Beth made for it again and again, snarling and yapping, forcing it down to the others who stood there stupidly, waiting to be terrorised.

The six animals were nearly at the oil drums and Robert watched in fascination. It was very quiet, there was only the faint rustle of the hedgerow, an odd bleat, birds twittering. Then the day exploded as something tore past his legs and careered about madly in the middle of the field, barking rapturously. Rags.

The sheep scattered hopelessly. Beth barked and ran off disconsolately to Morgan, her tail down. He picked up a stone and flung it hard, hitting Rags in the middle of the back. The mongrel yelped loudly, then did a complete tail-chasing circle in the middle of the field before shooting away again, past Robert, back towards the farm.

Morgan sat down and fussed the collie for a minute, then looked up. The sunshine poured down steadily, the sky was gloriously blue. After a while he got up heavily from the grass and ordered the dog to start again, shouting the queer strangled cries and clapping his hands. This time she got them down to the improvised fold more quickly and was nudging them towards the opening. Then Robert held his breath. Rags was back, and sniffing at his heels.

He shot out a hand to grab the dog's collar, but it was too late. He was already well down the meadow, and into the middle of the frightened sheep. The fencing fell part and one of the oil drums started to roll very slowly down the grassy slope.

This time Morgan didn't shout, but picked something up from the long grass and raised it to his shoulder. He said 'Rags,' just once, in a wheedling kind of voice. And the dog trusted him. It pricked up its ears and sat up begging, wagging its tail.

The sun flashed on a bar of silver. Robert cried out 'No, please, *don't!*' But the shot drowned him. The dog leaped quite high in the air crying hideously, then hit the ground writhing and twitching. Morgan fired again, and Rags lay still. The farmer did something to his gun then followed the collie over to the patched heap that lay small and bleeding in the middle of the great meadow. He hardly looked down, but walked rapidly to the gate, to where Robert was crouching down in some tangled bushes. The boy looked at his face as he lumbered past. It was swollen and puffy, the features coarsened and almost swallowed up in layers of fat. But his mouth was trembling.

Robert stayed where he was for a long time, just in case Morgan came back, but at last he heard the car doors banging and looked up to see a bright blue lozenge, the estate-car roof, flashing in and out of the hedges that bordered the track down to the road.

He walked into the middle of the field and looked at Rags. The dog might have been asleep. Its back was curved into an oval, its four paws were neatly together. But the one brown eye stared up at him. Robert stretched out a shaking hand and closed it quickly.

Morgan had shot it twice in the head; there were two small holes under the left ear and blood trickled from them very slowly. The dog was still soft and warm but already its body had that terrible flatness about it which he associated with death.

He'd touched the dog once but now his fingers froze. He pulled off his T-shirt and wrapped it round Rags, trying not to look at the head, then carried him over to the hedge. There was a deep ditch grown over with coarse grass and he laid the dog in it gently, covering him up with the T-shirt. The grass sprang up again, lush and sweet-smelling, hiding its pathetic secret.

He walked slowly along the edge of the field with the sun on his naked back and saw another car, a red one, bumping up the rutted track to the farm. Then he started to run and only slowed down when Aunt Em's cottage came in view. The countryside was very still and the voices of his family floated down from one of the fields. Then he heard another voice, sharper, more plaintive, repeating the same name over and over again, Gareth calling home his dog.

CHAPTER TEN

It was hot, the best day of the whole week and they were going home tomorrow. Mum was making her usual doorstep sandwiches for lunch which they were going to eat in the garden. Between them Dad and Idris had scythed the long grass, then mown it. It looked almost like a lawn again.

'I don't want to go home,' Ping said. 'Not *ever*.'

'What about Sally? And the youth club?' Robert said curiously. She was always very passionate about her friendships.

Ping pulled a face. 'I've been thinking about that. She didn't write to me, and I'd given her the address. I've gone off her a bit. Anyhow, I get bored with all that table tennis.'

Robert smiled inwardly. This sounded quite hopeful. She'd been nicer before she'd gone religious, someone he could talk to. He quite wanted to tell her about the Parrys. She'd done a very long topic on them and she'd read the whole of Mum's book about the border fights, too. He wanted to ask someone else if his theory about Aunt Em's cottage having been a Parry house sounded too crazy for words, and Ping would be sure to tell him. She had 'views' on everything, and she was rather clever. If there had been a Parry house on this site the murder story could have some truth in it. But *who* could have been murdered? And *when*? And *why*? He couldn't really tell her that bit. She'd start having nightmares about what might have been sealed up, behind the 'false' wall in his room.

He said 'I don't want to go, either.' How could they? He'd found the Parrys and what Gareth Morgan had been doing to them, and now Rags had been shot for going in with the sheep. Everything was unfinished.

'Hope Aunt Em stays in New Zealand.' Ping bit viciously into her first sandwich. 'I love this house.'

He loved it too. How could they go back, to the noise and smells of Buckden Heath?

Robert just couldn't eat. When he tried to swallow the food swelled to a hard lump in his throat. He kept seeing Rags sitting trustingly for Morgan to shoot him, and the horrible twitching, and the flies starting to settle. Even the smell of the food made him sick.

'Anyone want these? I'm not hungry,' he said.

Suddenly, somebody opened the little iron gate between the garden and the side field. Gareth was standing there, his usually ruddy face anxious and pale. He said at once, as if they'd never met before, 'Have you seen my dog?'

Dad got up from the grass. 'He's not been round this morning, though we do see him, now and again. Don't we Robert?'

His voice, harder, prodded the boy into life.

'Well, yes, sometimes,' Robert said numbly. He was looking down at the grass, not wanting to meet Gareth's eyes. But Ping was staring at him stonily. She'd not forgotten how Gareth had laughed and sneered at them, when they'd first tried to be friendly.

'My Gran said he was up home when you came this morning.'

'He was. He was under your car.'

'Can't understand it. He'd not been fed when I went to Llandewi. He always waits for me. I give him his breakfast.'

'He's a bit of a wanderer, isn't he, your dog? Perhaps he's gone off to get his own breakfast?' Dad grinned at Gareth but he didn't smile back. He stood there looking at the Elliotts spread out on the grass, dark and troubled, separate.

Mum said, 'Why don't we help you look for him? There are five of us. Surely, if we all come —'

'I'm not coming,' Ping said quietly.

'Listen, I think we're a bit of a crowd, love,' Dad interrupted. 'Mr Morgan may not want us all traipsing over his land. Why don't you two go off now, and start looking? You'll probably find him. If not I'll get the car out, and we'll do some driving round.'

'You coming then?' Gareth said stonily to Robert, when he didn't budge. 'Two's better than one.'

Unable to think straight, Robert got up from the grass and followed him.

They wandered over Morgan's land for about an hour. There were certain specific places Gareth went to first: a small smelly pool that Rags liked to wallow in and two shallow shafts where a small dog might get trapped, and be unable to get out. When he wasn't in either of them the search became rather aimless, but Gareth kept on calling and at one point he thought he'd found him, lying in a distant field. When they got there they found that the 'dog' was a big brown carton, sodden with rain. He kicked at it savagely and turned away.

'Why don't *you* shout him?' he said desperately to Robert. 'You're not doing much. He knows your voice as well. He might just come, for you.'

And Robert did call him, a thin bleat of hopelessnes for something terribly dead, that was lying in a ditch in the next field.

Everything was slowly becoming unreal. He should have told him straight away, in the paddock, with the family there. Mum would have known what to say to him. Anything would have been better than this. It was horrible when a pet died, they'd lost a dog and two cats on their busy main road but at least they'd had each other, and they'd been able to cheer each other up.

Who did Gareth have? His mother was dead and you couldn't exactly include Morgan, not when he'd fired the gun at Rags. Gran was lovely but she was old and frightened, and she'd keep out of it, for the sake of peace.

Gareth Morgan had no-one. That little dog had been his very best friend. He was pacing about more anxiously now, shouting louder, biting his lower lip. Robert couldn't stand it any more. He'd got to tell him.

They'd done a complete circuit of the fields and come back to the meadow where it had happened. He found himself clutching Gareth's arm.

'Gareth,' he said, 'Gareth, I . . . Rags is dead. Your father shot him, this morning. I was here. He was chasing the sheep again.'

The boy looked at him in disbelief, and then his face turned dead white. His lips worked strongly and he opened his mouth but no words came out. Robert said helplessly, 'I'm sorry, I'm really sorry. I should have told you at once, when you came to the cottage, but I, well, I mean, I didn't . . . I couldn't . . .' And his voice dried up impossibly.

Gareth said nothing. He stared hard at the ground then his face flushed red and he screwed his eyes up. Robert didn't speak either. They just stood together in the middle of the great green meadow, and the wind rippled the grass up to them, like silk.

'Wht did my dad do with him, then?'

'Nothing. When he'd gone I wrapped him up and put him in the hedge over there.'

Gareth walked in the direction of his finger till he reached the ditch, then he dropped to his knees and carefully undid the white bundle. Robert didn't follow. He turned away and looked blankly at the peaceful spread of fields and hills, the gleam of Aunt Em's cottage far below, under the big sky. He tried not to listen to the boy's crying but in the end he couldn't bear it. He walked slowly round the edge of the field till he got back to the gate, then sat there waiting.

At last Gareth came back with the T-shirt under his arm. 'There's blood all over this,' he said. 'I hope your mam won't get on at you.'

'Oh, forget it. She never notices things like that.'

They both leaned on the gate and stared across the grass. But Gareth's eyes were dead, like the eyes of a blind man.

After a moment Robert said awkwardly, 'I'm sorry I didn't tell you, but our dog got run over last year. It was terrible, and somehow I couldn't . . .'

'It's OK, just leave it, will you.' He scrubbed at his red eyes with his fists and turned on to the track, then they started walking down together.

As Robert stepped into the lane to go home Gareth turned back up the farm track, but he didn't stride out. He just stood there dumbly, his body limp as grass.

Robert had wanted to tackle him about the Parrys. He'd not forgotten about the rats, and the setting fire to the grass, and how the old man had trembled, huddled in his dark corner. But how could he start on all that now? He'd never in all his life seen anyone look so unhappy as Gareth Morgan did at that moment.

'Listen, why don't you come back with me?' he said suddenly. 'It's our last day here. We're not doing much, just messing around.'

Gareth shook his head, but he didn't actually move off.

'Go on, come back to our place. Don't go home and be on your own. Nobody'll mention R – your dog.' It helped not to say the name.

The boy shook his head again and Robert waited for him to walk off.

Instead he muttered 'What'll your dad say, and your mam, if I turn up?'

'Nothing. They'd be pleased.'

'Well . . . OK.'

When they got back to Aunt Em's Gareth hung about nervously in the paddock while Robert went into the house. His parents were in the big room and there were frustrated shrieks from upstairs where Nick was plaguing Ping. She was enshrined in her bedroom, mournfully tidying it up before they went home.

When they heard about Rags they exchanged one of their looks, then Dad whistled slowly through his teeth, something he only did when he was really angry, or shocked, and couldn't get any words out.

He'd heard them talking about Morgan in the village pub last night, when he went down with Idris. They'd all been chewing over his threatened court action, about the lonely valley property that he claimed was his. It had been in the local paper again. The land actually belonged to some pathetic old man, according to Idris, with a son who was too feeble to stick up for his father's rights. 'Unhinged,' the little Welsh man had said, grimly supping his pint. 'He's lived on his own too long, he should have remarried.'

Unhinged. Caught on the raw, a man like that might just shoot an uncontrollable dog. . . . But when it was his son's *pet*?

'You won't say anything about Rags, will you, Dad?' Robert said anxiously. His father's dark brooding look had a certain familiarity. What if he went straight up to Reg Morgan, and had it out with him? He was frightening when he really lost his temper.

'Well of course I won't. Don't be *ridiculous*.'

'And you won't let Nick say anything, or Ping, will you? He's really upset.'

'Wouldn't you be? Listen, nobody'll say a single word. Now go and get him to come in.'

Gareth came, reluctant and silent, but it was a good day in the end. They were just boys together, messing about. Nobody mentioned Rags, or the rats, or Reg Morgan, although Ping didn't make much of an effort to be friendly. She lay on her bed reading most of the day, and when Robert tried to get her to come outside she told him to go away.

They found some old scythes in the barn and Gareth managed to sharpen them up, and showed Robert how to use one and how to get the proper cutting rhythm. They stuck at it for most of the afternoon and cut down a lot of the long grass in the first field.

When Nick appeared, the scything turned into a general grass fight and they chased each other round the paddock, stuffing handfuls down each other's necks. Then they made a den. Robert had been promising to build something for Nick all week but it hadn't come to anything. They found two big pieces of corrugated iron and made it at the end of the paddock, between two tree trunks. It collapsed twice, with Nick in it, but in the end Gareth made it secure with an old door. He promised Nick a curtain entrance, if he could get a sack.

By tea-time the little boy's eyes were bulging with hero-worship. He thought Gareth was great and he kept trailing round after him. Robert heard him say, 'Robert wouldn't make me a den. I like you. I'd like you for a brother,' and he saw him hold Gareth's hand.

For a minute he felt jealous. If only he knew everything he might not be so friendly. Then he saw Gareth smile at Nick. It was the first smile Robert had seen, and he saw too how he held on to Nick's hand, as if he didn't want to let it go.

All day Gareth had been like a rubber band, stretched and stretched, till it must surely be at breaking point. And when Robert took a private look at him he saw, most of the time, that he seemed about to cry. He daren't talk to him yet, not about the Parrys, anyhow.

When Nick was put to bed he howled because Gareth was still downstairs. Dad had rung the farm number twice but nobody answered. On Saturday nights, Gareth told them, his Gran always went down to Groeyurgoch, to catch up on all the gossip with another old woman. His father would be at the Punch Bowl in Llandewi; he didn't drink locally.

By nine o'clock everyone was ravenous and there was no food in the house, apart from the ubiquitous cornflakes. Mum had 'run it down' she said, since they were going home in the morning. 'But I've had a brilliant idea,' she told them. 'What about that fish and chip van that stops in the village on Thursdays and Saturdays? Do you think it'll still be there, Gareth?'

'Should be,' he said gruffly, looking at his watch. 'They don't usually pack up till ten.'

Dad stood up. 'OK. Robert and I'll go. I'm taking orders.'

'Fish and chips all round, I should think,' Mum said, 'with plenty of salt and vinegar.'

'Just chips for me,' Ping informed him. She'd come out of her bedroom in the end, and joined the others by the fire. But she'd still not spoken to Gareth. 'Mushy peas too, if they've got them,' she added, 'but not if they're that bright green colour.'

'They're not,' Gareth said defensively. 'Everything's home-made on the van. Chamberlain's chips are great.'

Robert climbed into the car feeling hungry already. Mum's chips were always a disaster, uncooked and soggy, or else carbonised splinters. Her mind never concentrated itself on cooking. As Dad came out of the front door he could hear her playing odd notes on the piano.

When they came back from the village his father stopped on the road to let him in at the front so the chips could go straight into the bottom of the Aga. As he went past the big room he heard someone singing. He peeped in and saw his mother at the piano and Ping on the window-sill actually listening. Gareth was standing behind the piano-stool, turning the music.

It was a boy's voice, not yet broken, clear and sweet, that rose up as easily and as naturally as larks do, from the low grass. And it was of larks that the boy sang, an old folk song they sometimes sang at school. But never like this.

> 'Dear thoughts are in my mind
> And my soul soars enchanted
> As I hear the dear lark sing
> In the clear air of the day.'

Robert stood in the doorway with the chips, looking at Gareth's head in profile. The boy sang on, lost in the music, and he saw that the hard little face, that he'd only ever seen in expressions of anger, or ridicule, or pain, was quite changed now. It had softened, and become more open.

His mother, too, was quite lost in what she was doing. She was a good accompanist, never playing too loud and drowning the singer. She made the jangly old piano sound like a Bechstein.

'Do you know this?' Gareth was saying, leaning over her shoulder and playing something with his right hand. 'It's the thing I'm doing for the Llandewi Eisteddfod.'

Mrs Elliott listened carefully. 'No, no that's new to me, lovie. Can you play it both hands?' and she slid to the end of the long piano-stool to make room.

Lovie. That was kept specially for family and only when you were little or, now he was much older, in pain or some kind of trouble. Hearing her use it for Gareth made something tighten in Robert's throat. She wanted, he knew, to put her arms around him and let him cry about the dog till he felt better. But he sensed that she knew better than to intrude. It was too early and Gareth was too raw. Mum irritated Robert to death sometimes but she was always right about the big things. He loved her.

The Eisteddfod song was in Welsh, haunting and high, with a bass part that sounded like a dark slow river, flowing through forests. Gareth's voice, marvellously clear, filled the entire room. On the window-seat Ping sat listening and Mum's small hand had crept up instinctively over the boy's shoulder. She sat motionless now, her head bowed; in her mind, no doubt, she was singing it with him.

Suddenly he broke off, stood up and looked round, his face pink and embarrassed. Robert moved away from the door, in case he was spotted. 'That's as far as I've got,' he said. 'It's quite hard.'

'I love it,' Mum said simply. 'I'm coming to listen to you win, at the Eisteddfod. What's it about? Is it a love song?'

'Well, sort of.'

'Hasn't it got a name?'

'In English it would be . . . the father's prayer . . . no . . . the father's *lament*. It's about an old man whose daughter has died. The words don't mean very much, well, they keep repeating themselves. What's the point of life, now she's dead, that kind of thing. It's quite modern. The composer lives near Holywell.'

What is life to me without thee
What is life if thou are dead?
– Do you know that at all?' and Mum sang a bit to him.

97

'Oh aye, my dad's got that on an old record. He used to listen to music a lot. I love that.'

Robert crept away and put the parcel of chips in the Aga. Then he started buttering bread. They obviously hadn't moved out of the big room since he and Dad had gone down to the village and, somehow, he felt he ought to leave them alone a bit longer. Mum and Gareth were really talking to one another now. With Mum, the boy sounded like a normal person.

He felt more confused than ever, about what to do next. Gareth Morgan definitely needed sorting out, he couldn't go on persecuting the Parrys and frightening that old man to death. Someone ought to say something to him.

And yet. The boy who seemed to get a kick out of scaring people with guns, and putting dead rats in their drinking water, was the boy who'd been singing so joyously, in such peace, in the very next room. How much was his father to blame for what he was doing? Robert could still remember that awful moment in the farm kitchen, the fear that had passed over Gareth's face when the huge shadow filled the doorway, the burning cheeks in the yard, over the mud-spattered boots. Reg Morgan had a definite hold over him. Perhaps he'd started the Parry thing through simple fear of what his dad might do, if he dared to disobey. Then perhaps, without his ever realising it, going there and spying on them had become a kind of hobby, something to fill his time up. Lonely people did all kinds of peculiar things, and Gareth Morgan was definitely lonely.

Robert ought to keep his promise to Daniel Parry and his son, today hadn't changed that. But what about Gareth himself? He'd looked so unhappy until tonight, when Mum had got him singing. Underneath, Robert felt he really wasn't very tough at all. He just wanted to help him.

CHAPTER ELEVEN

But he didn't see Gareth again for months. Dad now spent part of each weekend in the office and when he was at home he shut himself up in his workroom. Mum said Steeles were giving him enough work for two, now they'd sacked Fred. He was still trying to get them to pay him what they owed.

Everyone said they missed Aunt Em's cottage and Robert felt as if the air and the smells of the town were stifling him. At night the traffic noises actually seemed to hurt his ears. They'd never bothered him before but after the peace of Aunt Em's, the lorries rumbling along the Chester Road were keeping him awake now.

'I'm sitting on the lion's side this time,' Ping announced, getting into the car. It was late July and they were going to Wales for a whole month. Dad was planning to join them at weekends when he could, and have a few days' holiday at the end if the work eased off. The baby was due in mid September but they'd be back home and at school again before that happened.

Ping didn't see Sally any more, they'd had a big quarrel. Now she'd got a big crush on Miss Roberts, her form teacher. She came from Aunt Em's part of Wales and she was threatening to pay them a visit.

Robert hoped she wouldn't, she'd got thick hockey legs and a faint blonde moustache.

Miss Roberts obviously knew quite a bit about those fights on the borders though and she'd given Ping top marks for her 'Parry' project. That was why she wanted to sit where she could see the lion. Robert had forgotten all about the old stone statue in Church Stoken. To him 'Parry' meant the living, not the dead, the old man and his son in the forgotten valley.

'What are you going to eat then, Dad?' he'd asked his father, as they loaded the boot with suitcases. 'Mum's not exactly stocked up for you. The larder's empty.'

'Dunno, you tell me. I don't suppose she's thought about it. I can always go and cadge a few meals from Grandma.'

'If only we could eat just when we wanted to, like cows,' Mrs Elliott said dreamily, helping Nick into his night clothes.

'Cows still have to eat, though,' Ping reminded her. 'In fact, they eat quite a lot.'

They didn't get away till late but it was exciting travelling in the dusk. There was hardly any traffic and they could go fast and watch the countryside rush by, a series of pale silhouettes, backlighted by the soft summer darkness. Nick was enchanted to be wearing his pyjamas in the car and he irritated them all by jabbering endlessly in a very loud voice. In the end he nodded off to the drone of the car engine. Robert dozed too, thinking of the Parrys in their dirty hut, about Rags, and Gareth Morgan.

For the first few days they saw nobody from the farm, except Gran, shuffling down the road on her way to the village. Robert kept thinking about going up there to see Gareth, but his courage always failed him at the last minute. Ping still had her knife in him, which didn't help. She'd implied that his going off to Morgan's would somehow be disloyal, and Robert felt torn. Then one morning Gareth appeared in the paddock with something wriggling under his jacket.

It was hot. Robert was lying in the grass, with a book, when a rough tongue suddenly licked his face.

'Gerroff, can't you!' Gareth was saying. 'Give over, Jem.'

Jem was a tawny-coloured labrador puppy with huge golden eyes. All three of them were round Gareth in seconds, fussing over the tiny thing, and pulling at its ears. Even Ping warmed up a bit. She adored animals. Nick, lost in a forest of legs, grizzled miserably, trying to get a look-in.

'Stop whingeing Nick!' Robert snapped, prising his brother's fingers from the leg of his jeans, but Gareth had dropped down onto the grass, so that Nick could have a proper stroke.

'You can hold him if you want,' he said gently; 'he bites a bit, but it's only pretending. He'll not hurt you.'

Gareth seemed different now, more relaxed. Perhaps having the puppy with him helped. Jem liked Nick. He calmed down in the child's arms, and eventually stopped yelping.

'He likes me!' he called proudly, going off towards his den, 'I'm his favourite!'

'Where did the puppy come from?' Robert said, when they were on their own.

'My dad gave him to me, because of Rags.' He paused. 'He did that in a rage. He brought this one home a couple of days after, went all the way to Denbigh for it. It's got a pedigree,' he added proudly.

'But I don't get it. First he shoots your dog, then he gets you another.'

'Oh he's mixed up, my dad is,' Gareth said, in a detached kind of way. 'Mixed up about a lot of things, he is, like keeping me at home with him. Says he wants the family to stick together. Huh! Some family! That's why he won't let me change schools. I'd be able to stay in Llandewi with my auntie, if I went to the Cathedral School. I suppose he thinks I'd leave home.'

'And would you?'

The boy shook his head. 'No, I'd not leave him.' Then he added, 'I love my dad.'

This was so unexpected that Robert could think of nothing to say for a moment. He should understand, he loved his parents . . . but *Morgan*.

'What about that scholarship you won, though?'

'Oh *that*, well it was nearly two years ago now. I'd only have a year in the choir, if I went. Still like to go, though, for the music. Dad's against it, he wants me to take over from him on the farm. But I don't want to, I'm not that interested. He says there's no money in music, only in muck.'

'Couldn't someone make him change his mind? What about your auntie? Or your Gran?'

'Ne'er. Gran couldn't do anything, she's dead scared of him and she does what he says, always has. She only stays up here because of . . . my mam. She used to live in Llandewi, with my auntie.'

'Could you stay with them, I mean, if your Dad gave in? Is it a big family?'

'There's uncle and auntie, and my three cousins. It'd be a bit squashed, but they'd make room for me. It's a proper family,' he added, in a tight sort of voice. He'd gone bright red.

Robert was puzzled by this new side of Gareth Morgan. He'd been all ready to have a go at him and tell him what the Parrys had threatened, but he was being quite friendly. They'd noticed it the minute he'd come into the paddock with Jem. He didn't seem so suspicious of them all anymore.

Perhaps he'd just needed someone to show a bit of friendliness. Perhaps it was Robert's asking him back to Aunt Em's, and that day they'd spent together. Mum might have talked to him too, when he'd gone for the chips with Dad. But if she had she'd kept it to herself.

Could he be trusted, though? There was still something that Robert didn't like, the hard shut-in look he had sometimes, the long silences, not to mention those weird visits to the Parrys. He still wasn't sure.

'Like to see my room?' he said, trying to sound casual. He didn't want to tackle him out here, in the garden, and Ping, who'd retreated into a leafy corner with a book, kept staring at him, and scowling. It was getting embarrassing.

'OK.' Gareth said flatly, not seeming at all interested. But he followed Robert up the stairs all the same.

He'd started on the hole again and he was getting on quite well with it. Gareth had lived in that gloomy farmhouse on the hill all his life, according to Dilys, so he must know quite a bit about the Groeyurgoch area. He'd be one person to ask about this cottage, especially after what he'd said about a murder being committed here. Robert hadn't believed him when he'd first said it, he'd thought it was just a lie. Now though, after Idris's peculiar reaction, he wasn't sure at all. If something *had* happened here what else did Gareth know about it?

He squatted on the floor while Gareth sat awkwardly on the bed and looked round. Then there was a very long silence. Robert still wanted to know about the rats but he couldn't get the words out. Even though he'd got Gareth on his own patch he was too nervous. Instead he said, 'What happened the day we went home? I mean, after your Dad destroyed Rags and went off to Llandewi?'

Gareth stared at his knees. 'He got back very late,' he mumbled. 'Wouldn't speak to me the day after, just kept out of my way. He always does that. He's a bit of a coward, if you want to know.'

'But didn't you wait up for him, I mean, that night?'

'Sure I waited up for him, and we had a flaming row. I'm not scared of him any more. I told him I wouldn't do anything else for him and that if he threatened me again I'd tell them at school, about him hitting me and that. That did it.'

'And what did he do?'

'Oh nothing much. He cried, and I went to bed.'

'He *cried*?'

'Yeah, he cried. He often does when he's in that mood, you know, when he's had a few drinks, and he'd had a skinful that night. Don't know how he got home without killing himself.'

'Was it –'

'Anyway,' Gareth interrupted, 'I'm not doing anything else he asks me, it's finished that is. He knows it as well. I've told my Auntie Margaret and she's had a go at him.'

'Was it your idea to go up the valley and frighten those people?' At last he'd said it.

Gareth didn't answer at first but a flush crept slowly over his face and he kicked at the floorboards.

'It was, wasn't it?'

'Listen, you don't know the full story. You must have heard what my dad's like. I bet Dilys Preece has been talking to you. She's a right gossip.'

'Was it your idea about the rats? That was a sick thing to do, I think.'

The moment it was out Robert wished he'd not said it. Gareth's face had clammed up again and he got to his feet.

'OK. I'm going home. I'm not staying here and listening to that. You don't know what you're talking about.'

'*Don't.*' Robert grabbed his arm and pushed him down onto the bed again. He was stronger than Gareth. 'I want to know, that's all. I promised the Parrys I'd ask you. I'm not *blaming* you.'

'You liar. You are. Of course you are. And you're a bloody hypocrite. One minute you're as nice as pie, the next minute you're going on at me. It's none of your business.'

There was another long silence, but Robert still had tight hold of Gareth's arm and he couldn't shake him off.

'Let *go* of me, can't you.'

'No, not till you tell me why you've been trying to frighten them.'

But still the boy said nothing.

'Gareth . . . don't you realise how serious it is? I mean, you could be put in a borstal or something, if anyone found out. It's not . . . you're not . . . *playing.*'

'Never said I was,' the boy said at last, through

106

clenched teeth. 'Never said I was playing. It's my dad you want to talk to, not me.'

Robert removed his hand, half expecting Gareth to get up and make for the door, but he stayed where he was, staring down at the floor, his mouth trembling.

'What d'you mean?'

'He made me. You don't know what it's like, living with him. He's a maniac.'

'Made you what?'

'Go there, to them. He wants them off his land. He wants to sell it to Peele so he can build his dream bungalow. He's wanted it for years.'

'But why didn't you refuse? You're not a kid.'

'How do you know I didn't refuse?'

'Well, *did* you?'

'Listen, it wasn't like you think. At the beginning I just went to the valley on my own. It was nothing *he* said.'

'Why did you go?'

'I just wanted to see it, didn't I? He'd always gone on about those people, as long as I could remember, he said they were filthy, owed him rent, or something.'

'Do they?'

'No, don't think so. There's no proof at all that the land's his. But there's always been an argument over it, going right back. I just went to see for myself.'

Gareth wasn't looking at Robert or really talking to him. It was as if, now the lid was off, and he'd started, he wanted to re-live the whole thing. He talked fast, and loud, in a harsh monotone.

'I went quite a few times, through that crack in the rock, just to see. One day I climbed right down, to have a look at that shack they live in. And it *is* filthy – Dad's right.' His voice swelled suddenly. 'They live like pigs out there . . . they stink. They let a dog out and it bit me. *Look*.' He turned his sleeve up and showed Robert two pink marks on his lower arm. 'Their bloody dog did that. I had to have an injection and everything.' He gave an empty little laugh. 'Anyway, my dad reported it, and it had to be destroyed. Even after it had bitten me they both started throwing stones, dancing about on the grass outside that hut, yelling at me, as if they'd gone mad.'

'But you'd *frightened* them. What did you expect?'

'Huh. Well, they weren't the only ones. I was frightened an' all.' He rubbed at the scars and pulled his shirt sleeve down, buttoning the cuff.

'I still don't see why you had to do . . . what you did,' Robert said, but he was hesitating now.

'When I told him,' Gareth went on, 'my dad went mad, and he got really drunk that night, said someone should give *them* a scare. Perhaps they'd clear out of the valley then,' he said. 'It set me thinking, that did.'

'But if he was drunk –'

'And the next week I went back, just to see what they were up to. I was standing at the valley head, where the waterfall comes out. The younger man saw me, the son. I wasn't doing anything but he started yelling. It got me on edge.'

'What did you do?'

'Fired a couple of shots with my pistol, just into the air like. That shut him up, he disappeared like a frightened rabbit,' and the boy smiled slyly.

'But he was scared, Gareth, and his father's had a stroke. A shock like that might have killed him.'

'Listen, I wasn't *planning* on going back but my dad started on me. Peele had written to him about the land

108

again, he was getting stroppy, said couldn't he sort it out and that, but Dad was harvesting. He couldn't leave the farm but he said I could easily get to the valley through the rocks, he used to go through it himself when he was younger, with his mates. He said I could tell them a thing or two, it might just shift them he said. When I didn't want to he said I was chicken, after the dog biting me and that. Well I wanted to show him didn't I? I wasn't chicken.'

'And you started a fire?'

'Ne'er,' Gareth said scornfully. 'I just put a match to some dried grass, that's all. I had a drop of paraffin so I used that too. It was miles away from them, it couldn't have done anything. I stamped it out after a bit. Just wanted to put the wind up them didn't I?'

'What about the rats?' Robert said numbly. This boy was warped, his personality couldn't have developed properly. 'That was terrible,' he added. 'I don't care what you say.'

'Well, my Dad told me to do that, he said it'd shift them. It was his idea that was.' But his cheeks were scarlet now.

Robert wanted to believe him, wanted to believe that everything was the father's fault, that angry lonely man who'd spent too many years on his own, brooding about his dead wife and thinking innocent people were against him. In a fit of rage he'd shot Gareth's precious dog then, in remorse, spent pounds on a pedigree replacement, only days after. You could imagine someone who went to crazy extremes like that getting his son to go and frighten the Parrys, and the son doing it because he was scared, and angry on his own account, angry that life hadn't given him a better deal. Filling a water butt with dead rats wasn't the sort of thing you did when your Mum and Dad were at home at the end of the day, in a house where everything was safe and ordinary, where people loved you. But it wasn't like that for Gareth Morgan and it never had been. He must have spent long hours cooped up with his father, listening to his aggrieved, sour talk, making the man's fears and suspicions his own. Not everything was his fault.

'You don't believe me do you?' Gareth said stonily, 'you think they were my ideas, don't you? Well they weren't, it was my Dad gave them to me in the first place.'

'OK, I believe you. I just hope there's no more trouble with your father.'

'There won't be, he's definitely got the message, Auntie Margaret really let him have it. There'll be something else soon enough, something else he gets into his thick head, that's the way he is.' His voice was bitter and there was a weariness in it too. Robert felt sorry for him now. It wasn't the moment to tell him the Parrys had made their own threats. Anyhow, he had the feeling it really was over. The worm had turned.

'I asked you up here to show you something,' he said awkwardly. 'Nobody else knows about it.' Now he was going to show Gareth his hole he felt curiously excited. Showing somebody would make it real. 'Look.' He opened the wardrobe door and shone his torch into the hole. It was considerably bigger now, he'd worked hard on it all yesterday afternoon when the others had gone down to Dilys's. The thin pink plaster skin had gone completely and he'd actually uncovered a couple of stones, and started to chip away at the greyish cement that held them in place. When he'd tapped at them with his hammer he thought, for a minute, that the sound was different, not a solid noise but more like a muffled ringing as if a foot or so away, through layers of stone, there might be a space.

At first Gareth wouldn't look, but eventually he peered into the wardrobe, scowling.

'Good God! Look what you've done! Does your Dad know about this, or your Mam?'

'Of course they don't. Anyway, I can always plaster it up again, and emulsion the wall. No-one'll know.'

'What are you doing it for anyway? What's the point?'

Robert felt rather stupid when he said that. 'I – I dunno, really,' he stammered. 'I just thought it'd be something to do. My dad's an architect and he thinks part of this room's been sealed off, because of the damp. I just wanted to *see*. You never know what . . .'

Then he stopped. He wasn't going to tell Gareth anything else, or that he thought Aunt Em's cottage had got something to do with the Parrys. He might sneer.

But the Welsh boy was looking at the hole quite carefully. 'Can I get in for a minute?'

'If you want.'

Somehow he felt depressed. He still didn't really like Gareth Morgan all that much, he was too moody, and he wished now that he'd not told him about the hole. It had spoiled it.

Gareth was soon out again, staring hard at the false wall, and the mess of plaster and dust framed in the mahogany door.

'I don't think you'll find anything behind there,' he said. 'Even if it is hollow, and you do break through.'

'How can you be so sure?'

'There's a funny wall like that up home, in one of the

barns. It was just like this, sort of built into the roof. My dad always said he was going to pull it down, to get more storage space. One day him and Mick, the man who works for us, drove a big hole in it.' He sniggered. 'It nearly killed them, it was that thick.'

'Did they find anything, or was it filled in?'

'Just a lot of old rubble, and a long narrow space, like this would be. It smelt terrible, it was so damp.'

'And there was nothing in it *at all*?'

'Nope. It was no use anyway, being so wet, and such a funny shape and that. My dad said he'd wasted his time.'

Robert was crushed. He stared at the rubble, spilling out of the wardrobe, and wished he'd never started on the hole in the first place.

'If you don't believe me, come home and I'll show you.'

'I do believe you. I just wish I'd not wasted my time, that's all.'

Gareth shrugged, and looked a bit embarrassed, then he started picking at the plaster himself, pretending to be interested. Robert said, 'What about the murder then, the one you said happened here? Were you just having me on?'

'Nope,' Gareth repeated, but Robert couldn't see his face.

'Well, what about it?'

'It's just an old story, lots of people know about it.'

'So who *was* murdered? Was it long ago?'

'Oh yeah, way back. And I don't know who or why, no-one does, and that's the truth. Something funny did happen here, though. That's all I can tell you.'

'Well, my mother had never heard about it and

112

she's been coming here since she was a child,' Robert said doubtfully.

'You wouldn't tell a little kid a thing like that, would you? I mean would you tell your Nick? It'd give him the willies, he'd have nightmares. Any road,' he said, 'have you got any proper tools? I could get a couple of these stones out for you. Can I have a go?'

'If you want.'

Gareth made a selection from the toolbox Robert had brought from home and heaved himself up into the wardrobe. After a minute or so he stuck his head out. 'Give me a hand, will you, I think I'm doing it.'

'OK, but we'd better not make too much noise. They're only up the fields. They'll be back soon.'

They were squashed like sardines in the tiny space. Two chisels were now driven deep into the wall on each side of one of the stones.

'It's definitely shifted. Grab the handle. No, not there. Further down. *Here*. Don't cut yourself. Now push down when I push. *Now!*'

They bore down hard but the stone wouldn't budge.

'Move yours about a bit, it's loose on my side, but don't pull the blade out yet.'

'It moved then, Gareth, it definitely moved!' Robert said, excited in spite of himself.

'Right. Now let's push again, together. *Now!*'

Nothing happened for a minute, then there was a kind of gritty scraping noise and the stone fell slowly out of the wall between their two chisels, and crashed down onto the wardrobe floor. When the dust had settled Robert put his hand frantically into the deep hole. His knuckles crunched up against stone and

113

came away bleeding. He could see another boulder, rougher than the first. He pushed at it hopelessly but it was solid, and as cold as marble.

'There seems to be another wall behind this one,' he said in a small voice.

'And there'll be another behind that, and another behind that. What did you expect?' Gareth said indifferently.

'Well I think you're both very naughty,' a voice said behind them. Robert almost fell out of the wardrobe. He shut the bedroom door, and locked it, then grabbed Nick by the shoulder.

'Ouch! Gedoff! You're hurting me!'

'What are you doing here? I thought you'd gone for a walk? I thought you'd gone with Mum and Ping?'

'I did. I did. I got home first. They're coming.'

Robert could hear Mum's voice floating down the field. He sat down heavily on the bed and tickled Jem's silky ears.

'Well, that's it. He'll tell Dad. He can't keep anything to himself.'

'Thought you said you could always plaster it up again? You scared of your dad, or something?'

'Well, it's not our house, is it? It's Aunt Em's, and my dad's a bit touchy at the moment. He's very on edge these days, with my mother having a baby and everything.'

Gareth heard doors opening downstairs. There obviously wasn't much time. He said, 'Listen Nick, you're my friend aren't you?'

Nick beamed and nodded, snuggling up to him.

'Well, if you are, promise you won't tell anyone about the hole in the wall. I want you to promise me.'

'Why can't I tell?'

'Because it's a secret. Nobody's got to know, not yet anyway. If you promise not to tell you can . . . you can share Jem. How's that?'

'That's silly. How can we share him? We can't cut him up.'

'No, but when he's here he's your dog. He's only got to sleep at my house, because he's used to it.'

'All right,' Nick said slowly. 'Can I have him now?'

'OK.'

He went off down the stairs with Jem in his arms.

'Will he tell, d'you think?' Gareth said, as he disappeared.

'He might, or he may just forget about it, if nobody mentions it to him, and while he's interested in the puppy. But you never can tell with him. Perhaps I'll get some cement and fill the hole in anyway. Thanks for talking to him, anyhow. He really likes you.'

'S'all right. No point in getting into a row with your dad is there?'

They sat together in silence. The low room felt stuffy in the heat and after a minute, Robert got up and opened the window.

'You've got a lot of books,' Gareth said, looking round the bedroom properly for the first time.

'Have I?' There didn't seem so many, to Robert. 'Ping's the book-worm. She's brilliant. She's always reading, so's Mum. She forgets to make the dinner sometimes.'

Gareth said, 'I like your mam. You're dead lucky, you are.'

'What was yours like?' Robert said.

'I don't really remember. She died when I was a baby.'

'What happened to her?'

115

'It was in our kitchen. She was making the tea. If Dad hadn't been in the yard the house could have caught fire, so they said. She was frying something.'

'What was wrong with her exactly?'

'She'd had a bad head-ache the day before, that was all. It was a brain haemorrhage. She just collapsed and died. She went out like a light, my dad says. It was that sudden.'

'How come you know so much about it, if you were only little?' Gareth must surely be telling the truth about a thing like this and yet Robert still didn't trust him not to lie, to get sympathy.

'My Gran told me, she's my mother's mother. And he still talks about it himself sometimes. When Mam died he didn't say her name for a whole year. That's what Gran said, anyway.'

After a minute Robert said, 'Sorry.' Old Daniel Parry had told him about Gareth's mother, the same story exactly.

'It doesn't matter. I really don't remember her properly. Don't waste your sympathy on me.'

Robert didn't say any more but something his grandmother had once said came into his mind. 'What you've never had you'll never miss.' That wasn't quite right though: Gareth had never enjoyed any kind of family life and yet he still missed it, you could tell that, from the way he'd latched on to Mum.

There was another prolonged silence. Gareth was still looking along the bookshelves and Robert was staring blankly at the wardrobe door. He wasn't thinking about his hole but about what it would be like if Mum died, or Dad. Before meeting Gareth Morgan he'd never really thought about things like this but now he'd been forced to think about them. He was on

116

the edge of the country Gareth lived in, looking in, and seeing what death did to people, and awful separation, and years of loneliness.

He glanced at his troubled clammed-up face as they sat there on the bed in awkward silence and he felt very young suddenly, as young as Nick.

CHAPTER TWELVE

Before he went home, Gareth invited Robert up to the farm the next morning. 'My dad's selling sheep tomorrow,' he said, 'in Denbigh. He'll be gone all day. If you come I can show you our wall, the one they had a go at, and we can get ourselves fish and chips. Chamberlain's van comes to the village Wednesday dinner times. I've got that thing for your mam, too. I meant to bring it today but I forgot.'

'What thing?' After the prickly way Gareth had been behaving this sudden friendly invitation had taken Robert by surprise. He was suspicious.

'She said she'd like to see the song I'm practising, the one for the Eisteddfod. Miss Jenkins got a photo-copy done for her and there's a letter about it too, from Hugo Powell. I thought she'd be interested, he's quite famous he is, he does a programme on BBC Wales.'

Robert felt jealous. He and Ping had both started piano lessons when they were six. She'd just got a distinction in Grade 5 but he'd only ever taken one exam and he'd failed it. He could hardly play at all now and his singing voice sounded like a crow with a sore throat. He didn't like to think about his mother and Gareth Morgan making music together. It made him feel pushed out.

But when he thought about Gareth that night, in bed, he felt slightly ashamed. He'd always got Mum, all of them had, so why should he mind when she was giving a little bit of love to a boy who'd never had any? She'd be surprised, if she knew how he felt.

He'd definitely go up to the farm tomorrow. Gareth didn't just want to show him the wall, there were also some special prize-winning calves he'd seemed rather enthusiastic about. He'd said he didn't want to be a farmer, yet he was anxious to impress Robert with his father's achievements. It obviously wasn't all hate between them, it was more love-hate.

He got there at ten the next day, as they'd agreed, but nobody answered when he knocked and the kitchen was dark. Perhaps Gareth had had to go to Denbigh with his father after all. Why hadn't he phoned, though? Then he saw a note propped against a cornflakes packet on the kitchen table. The door opened when he tried it so he went in. *Please wait*, it said, *back soon*, G.

The kitchen was very stuffy and Robert wandered outside again and walked along by the side of the house, peering in at windows. The panes were filmed over with grime giving only half-glimpses of gloomy rooms and passageways. It looked an unloved kind of house, full of ugly brown furniture on which the dust lay thick, like dirty icing sugar.

At the end a window was open and he looked in. This was obviously Gareth's bedroom. It contrasted very sharply with the rest of the house: in here everything was clean, tidy and cheerful. There was a patchwork quilt on the bed and shelves filled with carefully-arranged objects, bits of stone and rock, little tins, a model aeroplane. Some sheets of music lay on a

119

stand and there was a framed photograph on the wall next to it. Robert shoved his head in at the window to see it better. It was a family group, Morgan tall and handsome with crinkly black hair, a woman smiling at his side with her hand on the shoulder of a young boy in shorts. The man was cradling a small baby in his arms.

A note clipped to the sheets of music said 'For Mrs Elliott' in neat red capital letters. He reached a hand through the window and brought them outside, sitting down on the grass in the sunshine to look at them.

The verses printed under the lines of music were all in Welsh and so was the title. But he remembered that it was supposed to be some kind of lament, something a father had sung for a dead child. A photocopied letter was stapled to the music. It was from the composer, Hugo Powell, to Miss Sian Jenkins, the young woman in the village who taught Gareth piano and singing.

Originally, Robert read, *I had planned a setting of the Thomas Williams poem* The Cry of Elisha after Elija. *Then I came across the Rachel Parry story in a new book of Clwyd Legends by David Lewis-Jones. Perhaps you know it? It occurred to me that something 'nearer home' may well arouse local interest at the Eisteddfod. I'll try to come and hear Gareth on the 19th. He sounds rather special.*

Robert looked at the poem. This at least was in English, '*The Cry of Elisha after Elija*' translated from the Welsh by R. S. Thomas –

> 'The chariot of Israel came,
> and the bold, beautiful knights,
> to free from his close prison

120

the friend who was my delight;
Cold is my cry over the vast deep shaken,
Bereft was I, for he was taken . . .'

As he read it, a sort of shiver went through him and
he could hear the sound of trumpets. It was fantastic.
Hugo Powell's 'Rachel' music was much gentler; the
piano part to that had reminded him more of water
flowing, and of a sobbing child. *Rachel Parry* . . . and
her story was *local*. Did Gareth know anything about
her? He ought to get hold of this book, 'Clwyd
Legends'.

He was still poring over the poem when he heard a
car door bang in the farm lane. Hastily he put
everything back on the music stand, brushed the grass
off his jeans and shoved his hands in his pockets,
trying to look casual.

'Sorry,' Gareth said, coming through the rusty red
gate. He was lugging a plastic carrier bag. 'Gran's in
the village with old Mrs Owen. She insisted on giving
me all these vegetables and it's taken me hours to walk
back with them. I only got a lift at the bottom of your
hill.'

'It's OK, I've not been here all that long. I thought
perhaps you'd had to go to Denbigh, with your dad.'

'Seen the calves yet?' Gareth said, dumping his
carrier bag in the kitchen doorway. 'They're real
beauties, best we've had for years, Mick says. Come
on, they're across the yard. I'll show you.'

Robert followed him round the farm rather mechan-
ically, looking at the various things Gareth showed
him. There were some pretty calves to inspect, in a
shed, then the big barn wall that Morgan had once
broken into, with the damp space behind it, and

121

Gareth's bedroom with all its things on display, the room Robert had already peeped into, like a spy. But he didn't really see anything. His mind was on what he'd just read.

Rachel Parry. Who was she and had she ever lived in Aunt Em's cottage? Had she, perhaps, met some grisly death there? If so, when? And at whose hands? If the Parrys had really been such great landowners they'd never have lived in a humble labourer's cottage like Castell. Or was it actually the site of another house, something much bigger and grander?

Dad had dug the garden over in their first week and he'd turned up a tiny bit of wall, near the back boundary, thick wall, wall that might once have been part of a house. He'd not taken much notice of it except to say that it could have been an old farm building or perhaps part of the cottage itself that had fallen in, and been abandoned. What if that wall marked the original Parry home?

Robert couldn't ask Gareth about the Rachel Parry story – not yet, anyhow, because he wasn't supposed to have seen the music, or Hugo Powell's letter. If Gareth would only hand it over he could say something. But he seemed much more interested in showing him the farm, and the music and the poem remained tantalisingly on the music stand.

They were just counting out the fish and chip money which Gran had left on the dresser when the telephone rang. Gareth spoke to somebody then put it down. 'It was your dad,' he said, 'you've got to go home, *now*.'

'*Dad*? But he's working this week, he's in Buckden.'

Gareth shrugged. 'It was definitely him. You'd better get off, he sounded in a bit of a state.'

Robert went to the door, wondering what on earth had brought Dad to Aunt Em's. Could Grandma Elliott have had another fall? His mother would want to go and see her, if she was in hospital again.

He said 'I'd better go, then. Everything was OK when I left this morning, I don't get it.'

'Do you want to take that music for your mam?' Gareth asked him. 'Hang on a minute, I'll go and fetch it.'

Robert shouldn't have waited but he wanted to get his hands on that letter from the composer and have a really good look at it before handing it over to his mother. She tended to put things 'in a safe place', then forget where the safe place was.

As he ran down the lane towards Castell he saw their car jutting out into the road, parked all crooked. It was behind someone else's, a large well-groomed vehicle, an old Rover. This first car had an unfriendly 'offical' look.

The house was uncannily quiet. 'Yoo hoo!' he called out, 'where is everybody?'

'In here, my darling,' a voice answered from the dining-room. But it wasn't Mum. It was Dilys Preece, sitting by the fire-place in his mother's chair, with Nick on her knee. They were doing cat's cradle with a bit of pink wool. Ping sat opposite, holding a book. But she wasn't reading it. Her face was all puffy and blotched, and it had that red smeary look you get when you have been crying for a long time.

'Where's Mum?' Something was obviously wrong, and it obviously was to do with his mother.

'She's gone to hospital, in an *ambulance*!' Ping said, and she burst into tears.

'Where's Dad?'

'In the big room, talking to the doctor.'

Robert went straight to the door.

'Don't go in,' Dilys said, 'they'll be out in a minute.'
But he went through all the same and eavesdropped
unashamedly. He couldn't make out much of what
they were saying, only words like 'full term' and
'blood pressure' and 'complete bedrest'.

'What's wrong, then? Mum seemed perfectly all
right at breakfast.'

'Now you're not to go worrying dear,' Dilys said
calmly, 'I've just been telling Ping, isn't it, pet? She
came over a bit faint, at about eleven it was. I was here,
thank God. We phoned Dr Davis at the surgery, and
he came straight up to see her, and –' She paused,
uncertain how to put it, with Nick all ears, 'and with
your new baby coming he thought it best if she went
into the cottage hospital for a while.'

'Is she having the baby now, then?' It was too early.
It'd be a proper baby and it might come out dead. He
wanted to be sick.

'Oh *no*, but she has to rest properly, in bed.'

'She could rest here,' Ping said hoarsely. 'We'd do
everything. She didn't have to go into hospital. I *hate*
hospitals.'

'Yes, why does she have to be there?' Nick said,
starting to cry. 'Why can't we have her in one of our
beds? I want her, I want *Mummy*,' and he howled
passionately.

And that's how Dad found them, Nick sobbing on
Dilys's knee, Ping staring dumbly into the fire-place,
Robert standing on the rag rug, with his hands in his
pockets.

He said, 'Thanks for taking over, Mrs Preece, it's
really very good of you.' His voice was flat and

expressionless yet Robert detected a certain edge to it.

He said nervously 'Er, does it mean we'll have to go home?'

'No it does *not*.' For some reason the question angered him. 'You're staying here as long as your mother has to be in the hospital. There's nobody to look after you in Buckden, and anyway, she wants you to have your holiday here just as we'd planned. She wouldn't even let me go with her to the hospital. Mrs Preece is moving in to look after you, it's all fixed up. Not that you deserve such consideration.'

'I only asked. Honestly, Dad. There's no need to shout. I mean, she's going to be *OK*. What is the matter with you?'

'I'll show you what the matter is.' Dad grabbed him roughly by the shoulder and pushed him upstairs. Robert thought he was going to hit him; then he was propelled up the steps into his bedroom.

It was transformed. The wardrobe had been pulled away from the wall and the rubble from the drawer was in a heap, on some newspapers. Now the hole was exposed Robert was amazed to see how large it had been. If there'd not been a second layer of boulders behind the first he could have got through.

But it would never happen now. He daren't go against his father in this mood.

'I don't know what the *hell* you were playing at Robert, I really don't, but this is just about the last straw. How could you make this appalling mess, coming up here in secret, doing all this damage, telling me lies, making me think you were somewhere else? It makes me wonder what you've got for brains, inside that head of yours.'

'But Dad, you said –'

'I don't care what I said, or what damn fool idea you've got. This is not our house, it's Aunt Em's. She's an old lady. She trusted us with it. How you could think you'd got any right to do *this* sort of thing I just don't know. Don't you think I've got enough to worry about, without this? Don't you think –'

He was interrupted by a mournful dog-like howl. Nick was in the doorway. Now he knew how Dad had found out.

'I'm sorry Robert, please don't shout at me. Daddy's shouting.'

'And you had no right to force him to make a ridiculous promise about keeping quiet, you and Gareth Morgan, bribing him with that dog. I'm disgusted with you. Just keep out of my way. You sicken me, you really do. Why can't you grow up? D'you think you're being the Famous Five or something? I'm going to see your mother now and just behave yourself will you, if it's not asking too much.' And he turned and went heavily down the stirs.

Robert could never remember his father being quite so angry before, or shouting quite so violently. It made him go cold inside. It must be because Mum really was ill, or in some danger even. Dilys couldn't have told him everything.

Nick was crying bitterly now, and Ping was no use. She'd barricaded herself in her room. When things really upset her she always disappeared. She didn't like showing her feelings in front of other people. Robert sat on the bed and gave Nick a cuddle. He kept saying 'Why is Daddy shouting?' and 'I want Snoopy' and 'I want Mummy', over and over again. It was no good explaining that Dad was worried about Mum, and that it wasn't really about the hole: that in another

126

mood he'd have laughed, and been interested. He'd have to think of a diversion.

'Let's get Ping and go to the den, Nick,' he tried, and then 'Let's see if Mrs Preece has got anything good to eat. She always makes nice things.' But Nick wouldn't budge, he just clung to Robert and howled, soaking the front of his jersey.

Robert felt like howling too. He loved Aunt Em's cottage now, more and more it felt like home. But it was going to be awful without Mum around. She'd only left them once before, that time Nick was born, and it had been awful then.

That was what the matter was with Dad. They all loved Mum so much. She was the warmth in the house, the heart of it. She was like the light in the window when he came home. He hated it here without her. He hated everything.

CHAPTER THIRTEEN

Dilys moved in next day and Dad went back to Buckden. Everything settled down remarkably quickly after that and very soon the new routine began to feel quite normal, almost as if there'd never been any other.

They all felt better when they'd actually seen their mother. Somehow Robert had feared a terrible deterioration, that she'd have become all wizened and death-like overnight, or else look as if she'd had a stroke, like the old man in the valley. But she was still Mum. Nick clambered all over the bed and she made them all giggle with stories about the fat bossy matron who terrorised all the nurses. Some days Idris brought them into Llandewi in his van but then Mum said they could come in on the bus if they wanted.

Living with Dilys wasn't quite like going down for tea now and again. She was quite strict. Meals arrived on time and you had to be sitting at the table ready. Breakfast was at 8.30 prompt. Robert detested getting up but there was nothing else for it, he'd got to be washed, combed and dressed by the time she arrived with his plate. She had an unfailing instinct for dirty nails and neglected backs of necks. In addition, everything disappeared into the washing machine the minute it was taken off.

'Honestly,' Robert grumbled one morning, hunting round for his favourite old sweater, 'she's absolutely obsessed with washing. I wish Mum was here.' It was one of those awful moments. Dilys, at the top of the stairs with the hoover, had obviously heard.

Ping came out of her bedroom and hugged her. 'What he means is that you're just too good at looking after us and anyhow, everyone knows how filthy and stinking boys are.'

Robert said awkwardly 'Sorry, Dilys. I know you've got a lot to do.'

'Ach, don't bother yourself. Just make your bed for me, darling,' and she shook a duster out of the nearest window, her round handsome face rather pink.

'Thanks,' he muttered to his sister, his own face crimson with embarrassment. If Ping didn't become a professor she'd be a top-flight diplomat.

Dilys spent part of each day at her own cottage and Nick often went with her. She used the old motorbike and sidecar which had belonged to one of her grown-up sons and she rode it in great style, roaring off down the hill with her old mack billowing out behind her. She slept at the cottage each night, and Dad came whenever he could. But Steeles were keeping him very busy and often he went in to visit Mum then had to drive back to Buckden Heath without seeing them. He phoned every night and spoke to all three of them but it wasn't the same.

The big room was banned. Dilys's first chore had been to clean it thoroughly for Mum's return and they weren't allowed in. It smelt unlived-in and cold, with its unlit fire and the abandoned piano. Nobody wanted to go in there anyway, not now.

It was at night they thought most about Mum and

129

Dad. Nick would go through the facts methodically in a loud voice, as if he was trying to get the pattern back into his ordered life, and straighten out the lines that had gone all wiggly on the day Mum had gone off in the ambulance.

Ping had gone very quiet. Miss Roberts never came on the promised visit though every morning she waited for a letter, or a phone call. Robert hoped she would, in spite of her moustache and hockey legs. Ping needed cheering up.

He spent quite a lot of time up at Morgans'. They were still haymaking and he went into the fields most mornings, to help. Gareth's Dad hadn't said a word to him so far, but at least he'd not told him to clear off.

Gareth knew now that the Parrys had made threats. 'It's up to you, whether you tell your father,' Robert had said. 'But they definitely dropped hints. "Two can play at that game", that's what Dan said.' Whether this information had been passed on to Morgan he wasn't sure. But there were no more references to the valley people, and Gareth certainly didn't go on any more secret expeditions. He'd said all that was 'over', and it did seem to be.

One dinner time, when Robert got back from the farm, he heard Ping crying behind her bedroom door. He knocked but she didn't answer so, after a minute, he went in.

'What's up?' He tried to put his arm round her but she shook it off. 'Nothing. Leave me alone.'

'There is. Don't be daft.'

Ping sniffed and rubbed her eyes violently. 'I just wish Mum'd come back, that's all. You spend all your time with Gareth Morgan though I can't understand what you see in him, and Dilys has got her work cut out keeping Nick amused. If we were at home at least I'd have people to see, but there's no-one here. I hate it without Mum and Dad!' – and she started crying again.

'Oh come on, Ping, it's not that bad. We see Mum nearly every day, and Dad's coming at the weekend. Cheer up, for heaven's sake.'

But he felt guilty. It was true that he'd been spending a lot of time up at the farm. Somehow he'd not thought she'd mind, being left at the cottage with Dilys. She'd never complained about him going off when Mum was there.

Mum wasn't there though, she was lying in a hospital bed, and although Dilys was very kind to them Ping obviously missed her mother as much as Robert did. He'd been glad to go up to the farm, just to get out of the empty house. She obviously felt its emptiness too. He'd been selfish.

If only Dad hadn't discovered the hole in the wall he could have broken through by now, and Ping could have helped him. She knew all about his 'Parry' theories, though she'd not seemed very convinced that there was anything behind them. He'd not mentioned the actual murder yet. He wanted to, but she had much too vivid an imagination, and if his father got wind of it he might go off into one of his rages again, and yell at him for frightening her.

There was one thing he'd decided to do about the wall, even though he'd had to fill the hole in. It was to track down this book called Clwyd Legends the composer of the song had mentioned, just to see if his 'Rachel Parry' song could in any way relate to *this* bit of Wales, and to Aunt Em's cottage.

So far, though, he'd drawn a complete blank. There

wasn't a bookshop in Llandewi and the little library didn't have *Clwyd Legends*, they said. The woman had suggested writing to the author. 'You never know,' she told him, 'he might even send you a copy.' So Robert wrote, but he got no reply to his letter.

'I'm fed up about that,' he told Ping. She'd consented to let him sit on her bed now, and she'd at last stopped crying. 'You'd have thought he'd be pleased that someone took the trouble to write.'

'Why don't we write to the composer?' Ping suggested. 'He'll have a copy, he must have.'

So they decided to write another letter and send it to Novello's music publishers, in London. The address was printed on Gareth's song which was still on the piano waiting for Mum's return. He'd visited her twice in hospital, and taken her a plant.

Looking at all the bits and pieces waiting for his mother to come back, made Robert feel sad. He knew nothing bad was going to happen to her, it was just the waiting. He shut the door on the big room with its cold museum smell and followed Ping into the kitchen where she was busy sorting through her italic nibs, at the big scrubbed table.

'I've had another idea,' she told him, as he got a sheet of paper and tried to work out what they were going to say to Hugo Powell. 'We ought to get that old man to let us take the ring to the Fire Station Museum. If they really are the same it's got to mean something. In fact,' and she put her pen down, 'we should do that first. It'd be solid proof.'

Robert had told her about the two men in the valley, the day Dad had blown his top about the wall. She'd seemed very doubtful at first but the song and the legend, above all the fact that it was the same name,

132

Parry, seemed to have convinced her that Robert wasn't just fantasising.

But he shook his head. 'He'd never let me take it. You don't know what they're like, they're . . . well, scared of everything. They'd think I was going to sell it.'

'If you'd take me to see them I could judge for myself, couldn't I?' Ping said rather acidly. 'But you seem to want to keep them to yourself, you and Gareth Morgan. I've never liked him, he's so . . . secretive.' She didn't know yet what Gareth had been doing at the Parrys. Robert kept quiet about that. He didn't want her to think even worse things about him. She was quite hostile enough already.

'Listen, I *will* take you to the valley,' he promised rashly. 'Only, well, not yet.' It was perfectly obvious to Ping that he didn't really want to. 'Now are you ready?' he said more briskly. 'Dear Dr Powell –'

'I suppose I am, though I don't see why I should write your letter for you,' she said frostily. She was definitely hurt again. Robert couldn't keep up with Ping's moods at all.

One day, after visiting Mum, they did some shopping in Llandewi for Dilys. Robert spotted a tourist map of the area, in a glass frame, in the High Street. It was new so they went over to look at it. He had planned a big walk for the Saturday, with Gareth; 'up the mountain' was how he had described where they were going, meaning the hilly moorland region, north-west of the hidden valley. 'Nobody ever goes there,' he'd said. 'It's great. My Dad'll be out all Saturday so we could go off for the whole day. Gran'll do us some food.' He'd not looked very pleased when he'd heard that Ping was coming with them. But Robert thought she had a point, complaining about being left at the cottage all day long; it was about time Gareth behaved like a human being towards her, in his opinion. She could easily have helped with the haymaking, for example, but he'd always pulled a face when Robert suggested it.

'OK, if she doesn't come, I won't come either,' Robert had told him. So Gareth had grudgingly agreed, but he looked very black, all the same, and stalked off.

They were still looking at the new map when someone came up and spoke to Robert. He turned round and saw Dan Parry, the old man's son. It was odd seeing him in Llandewi High Street, where toddlers were grizzling for ice-cream and somebody was arguing about change. He wore the same old suit, held together with safety-pins, and a dirty scarf knotted round his neck. He smelt funny, too. Ping stepped back a little, and gave him one of her stares.

'You never came back,' he said rather accusingly.

'No, but I didn't forget, I did tackle him about it and I told him what you said as well, that two people could play at that game. He's not been back since, has he?'

'No. But his Dad's still on at us.'

'What's he doing now, then?'

'I've just been to the welfare, haven't I?' and he thumbed at some council offices across the street. 'Morgan's been on to them now. Wrote them a letter. They came to see us and said we've got to get out. No proper sanitation, they said, too damp. Should be condemned, they said, and my Dad's got to have a nurse looking in. Well, they can stuff that.'

'Are you sure it was Morgan who put them on to

you?' But Robert knew it must be. He tried to imagine Daniel Parry and his father being uprooted from their valley, and going to live in a bright modern flat, in the town. He couldn't. It'd kill them.

'I'll try and come,' he said. 'I'll bring Gareth with me.'

'What good would that do?'

'Well, you never know, perhaps he could speak to his father. Anyway, Ping, my sister, she'd like to come and see the – where you live. We were just looking at the map, we're going for a walk the day after tomorrow. We could come then.'

'If you'd let me borrow that old ring,' Ping said suddenly, 'we'd take it to the museum for you. We've been . . . I've been doing a school project on the history of the Parry family, and I've got to know the man in charge. He's nice. I bet he'd know all about it, what it's worth, and everything.'

'My Dad'll never sell it, if that's what you're getting at,' Dan grunted.

'No, but I'd bet he'd be interested in its history . . . *You* could take it to the museum if you'd rather. Mr Rowlands, the man's called.'

'Ne'er, I'm not going in a place like that,' but they could see that the idea interested him.

'Listen, we *will* come, Dan,' Robert said. 'I've still got your flash-light, anyhow. We're setting off quite early so allowing for stops, (Ping would slow them up and he was already worrying about Gareth's reaction) . . . I should think we'd see you about four o'clock. Or say half past, OK?'

'OK. My Dad won't part with that ring, though,' – and he walked off, muttering.

CHAPTER FOURTEEN

On his own, Robert would have enjoyed the walk. The country wasn't lush or pretty but the barren wilderness of treeless moorland excited him much more. It hadn't rained for weeks and everything was dried-up and brownish. Sometimes their path crossed streams which were only trickles at the bottom of rocky beds. And the quiet was uncanny. He could count the birds they'd seen, and there were no sheep grazing.

The dark hump of a mountain called Moel-y-bryn lay squarely at the end of the long straight track they were following. He would climb it one day, this was his country. It was as if he'd just met somebody he liked very much and was thinking, All those years we've been living in Buckden Heath and you were only at the end of the next road. All those years he'd been alive and thought of Aunt Em as a fussy old relation who knitted sweaters and forgot your birthday. And she'd lived here, and had this.

But Gareth was spoiling it. He'd made it obvious from the very beginning that they shouldn't have brought Ping and he walked much too fast for her, scowling and swearing under his breath whenever she dropped behind. Now she was sitting down again, the second time in an hour, rolling her sock back to inspect her heel. Her sneakers were new and they were rubbing. Underneath the skin was bright pink and very watery. 'That looks sore,' Robert said. 'Let's put a plaster on it. I've got some.'

'Will he mind waiting?' Ping whispered nervously, looking at Gareth's back. He was standing on his own with his hands in his pockets, staring at the sky. 'He's so moody, and I can't go any faster, I just can't. I told Mum these were too tight when she brought them home.' Her eyes had filled with tears now and she stared hard at the grass, pulling bits out.

'It's OK, don't you bother about him. He nearly couldn't come anyhow, because of his dad. It's put him in a bad mood, that's all. Come on, put your sock back on.'

Then he went over to Gareth. 'We can't go back the way we planned,' he whispered, 'it's too far for Ping.'

'What d'you suggest, then?' the boy said irritably.

'Well, we could leave this path up *here*,' Robert said, with his finger on the map, 'and get to the rocks where the passage is. Then we could walk down on to the bottom road . . . here . . . and thumb a lift to the village.'

'You're trying to get me to talk to the Parrys, aren't you?' Gareth said suspiciously.

'No, I'm not. But what harm would it do if you did see them? It might even do some good. You owe them something, after putting the wind up them like that.' He'd not told Gareth about his promise to Dan, in case he backed out of the walk altogether. Somehow, though, he was determined to get him to the valley.

'With my dad on at them, through the welfare? What'd they think of me?'

'You could have asked him to stop harassing them, Gareth. At least you could have tried.'

'I *did* ask,' Gareth shouted, 'I *did* ask. He just told me to shut my face, said I didn't know what I was talking about. That's what he's like. You get nowhere with him.'

'Well OK, you can tell them you've *tried*, at least. Anyway, we'll have to take a short cut somehow, she's crying. She's only ten, you know. And I've got their torch,' Robert ended desperately. 'I said I'd take it back. I met Dan in town on Thursday. He's expecting me and I'm going.'

Meanwhile Ping had scrambled up a stone-littered slope to where the land flattened out in a long swathe of dried-up grass. She'd privately decided to ignore Gareth Morgan from now on. He wasn't worth bothering with. 'Isn't it funny here,' she called to her brother. 'It's like a sort of . . . a sort of *moonscape*. Look at these circles.'

He came up the slope while Gareth stood on a boulder, staring across at them coldly. You could see something had happened here, long ago. Holes had been dug in the ground, then filled up, but afterwards the land had sunk, making rough crater shapes under the grass. With the land so dried-up the rings and whorls on the moor's pitted face could be seen very clearly.

Robert noticed groups of old fence-posts here and there. 'It's where they sank shafts, I suppose, years ago. D'you remember Idris telling me about it? There'll be holes inside those posts. Funny place to do it, out here.'

'There must have been a lot of them,' she said,

walking further on. 'Ugh, there's an enormous one here, and a horrible smell.'

'Don't go nearer than that, Ping. They're dangerous.'

'I'm *not*.'

But she was feeling the grass with her fingers. 'It's all soft here, and short, there *must* be sheep somewhere. And it's so springy, look!' She'd started to jump up and down gently. 'Ooh, it feels lovely, it's rubbery, like a trampoline!'

Robert had joined her and was kicking at the grass, squashing it down with a heel and watching it spring back. The smell from the shaft was foul, like bad meat, and he thought of that sheep's skull Idris had shown him, grinning up inanely.

Then it happened, just as Gareth came up the slope to them, his face suddenly sharp with worry. 'Stop doing that, stop it, you bloody fools. It's not safe –' and he made a grab at the cavorting Ping who was much too near the mouth of the shaft.

But the whole earth seemed to have lurched sideways and he was too late. He was suddenly tipped towards Robert and their skulls crashed together. The posts round the shaft seemed to turn into a bundle of matchsticks uprooted from the soil, for the earth itself seemed to be moving.

Ping screamed and found there was nothing under her feet. The grass had split in two and she was falling, they were all falling, in a helpless tangle of limbs. Sharp walls tore at them and earth fell on their faces and into their eyes, and they were being hurled down, twenty, thirty feet, landing in mud at the bottom of a great hole, in a terrified, bleeding heap.

She went on screaming. The others were dumb.

Dust swirled up over their heads, gossamery into the sunlit air, then a bird started twittering, excited by the strange activity of falling earth and stones in its unpeopled quietness.

They listened. Seconds later the bird-song died also, and they were left alone, in a huge and terrible silence.

At first there was only the darkness, their three bodies crushed up together and the damp earthy smell of the shaft. Robert's lips were dry but when he licked them he could taste blood. He must have gashed his chin on the rocky side of the hole, as they fell. Gareth's left ankle was twisted under him and a dull pain throbbed through it. It felt limp and useless and he knew it must be sprained or broken. The one movement he'd made had sent pain shooting through it, pain sharp enough to make him gasp. He wasn't telling those two, though.

Ping's crying turned at last into a dry sob, not loud, but still the shaft echoed with it. As their eyes adjusted to the gloom they looked at each other slowly, then they all stared up.

It was three o'clock on a fine day in midsummer and the world over their heads was warm and windless. They could see a rough circle of light, flat blue-grey, bisected once or twice by old metal posts. Very slowly their eyes travelled down, along the shaft walls, through the two dozen feet of earth and rocks, till they reached the bottom, and looked at each other again.

'We must have been on a kind of overhang,' Robert whispered. 'Just a thick bit of turf with nothing underneath. This must be part of some mine workings that they'd not filled in properly, or something.'

'You shouldn't have gone near it, anyone could've

told you that. You should've kept away. What d'you think the bloody posts are there for?'

'Well, you could have *told* us,' Ping said, starting to cry again. 'If you'd not gone off, if you'd have seen what I was doing . . .'

'Now you listen to me, you little bitch . . .'

'Shut your mouth, Gareth Morgan,' Robert said suddenly. 'You as well, Ping. Just dry up, both of you. It's happened now, and we are in it together. We're not *dead*. How're we going to climb out, that's what I want to know.'

'We can't,' said Gareth flatly. 'We're much too far down. Unless you're a miracle worker, or something.'

Robert had fallen with his rucksack on his back. He took Daniel Parry's flashlight out of it and shone it round the hole, hoping desperately to find some kind of passage that might slope upward and take them high enough to clamber out. But there was nothing. They were at the bottom of a very deep shaft. There was only the crack in the side, filled now with fresh earth and rubble, that led through to the other great hole, where the decomposed animal must be. He was beginning to smell it already, through the moistness of the freshly-fallen soil.

'Have you ever heard of someone getting stuck down one of these?' he said to Gareth, sounding calmer than he felt. 'There must be some way we can get out.'

'Now and then,' was the sullen reply. 'Sheep do, all the time. They don't always find them in time, though.'

No, the sheep I saw didn't make it, Robert was thinking, and Gareth thought of the story of the shepherd, Ivor Pritchard, who'd gone missing, twenty years ago, and who was found weeks later, in a shaft on their own land, stinking and unrecognisable.

'Listen, we'll have to try and make some kind of a rope,' he said suddenly. 'What have you got in your rucksack?'

Robert tipped the contents out, onto the mud, and shone the torch. There was the remains of his packed lunch, a pen-knife, and an old towel wrapped round a bit of soap. Dilys had put that in. As if you'd stop to wash on a hike.

'We'll have to use the towel, and our T-shirts. Help me off with mine, will you?'

But Gareth didn't move, and all the colour had drained away from his face.

'What's the matter?' said Robert. 'There's room to stand, just about.'

'I can't put my weight on my foot, if I –' Gareth did try to stand up. Then he screamed.

In the wobbling torch-light Ping saw his face, white with the pain, his teeth over his lower lip. Then she too could smell the dead sheep; she knew what it was immediately.

'Gareth,' she said in panic. 'What's the matter with you? What's wrong with your foot? Let's put something wet on it, the earth's wet.' She was still crying, but quietly, and she stopped as she carefully scooped up the mud then patted it on to his foot and ankle. 'It's that smell, if only we couldn't smell *that*,' she said.

'Why don't you have a sniff at this soap?' Gareth said faintly. 'It's lemons.'

'Good idea,' Robert said, putting it into her hand. They all felt a bit better, then, not so frightened, for a moment, and Gareth was gentler.

142

'What use would a rope be, even if we had got one?' Robert said.

Gareth pointed up the hole. 'Well, we could try and hook it round one of those posts, it might hold. Then one of you'll have to try and get up it. Don't think I can.'

'But we'd never manage that,' Robert said. 'We're too far down. How could we get a rope round one of those? You're crazy.'

'OK,' Gareth threw the pen-knife down angrily. 'It was only a suggestion. You think of something, if you're so damned clever.'

But Robert couldn't. The sides of the shaft just crumbled away when you stuck the knife-blade in, you couldn't make footholes, and anyway it was absolutely sheer. He could feel Gareth glowering at him as he hacked away pathetically. In the end he gave up.

'All right. How do we make a rope, then?'

Between them they had three T-shirts and Dilys's old towel. Soon they were laid out on the mud at the bottom of the hole.

'D'you think it'll be long enough?' Robert said doubtfully.

'Well it's got to be. But we can't make the pieces too thin, or it'll tear.'

'I'll climb up it,' Ping said. 'I'm much lighter than you two.'

Cutting everything into strips with a small blunt knife took about an hour. There was no room to move their arms about properly and the cramps in their legs were terrible. In the end Gareth knotted it all together. It was quicker if one person did everything, and he seemed to know exactly what he was doing. Robert tried to help at first, but his hands shook too much. Gareth made a loop at the end and passed the 'rope' through, then everyone looked up. It wasn't nearly long enough but there was nothing else to add to it. All three were naked and shivering under their sweaters, as the dampness struck through them. Over their heads the thin shattered post spiked the disc of light. The sky was fading now from blue to pearl, from pearl to deep rose.

Robert coiled the ragged rope in his hand and stood on his toes.

'You'll have to stand on my shoulders,' Gareth said, 'or you'll get nowhere near it.' He straightened up very slowly, wincing at the agonising pain in his ankle.

'Let's have a look at your foot first,' Robert said, shining the torch on it. Gareth turned his sock down. It was like a balloon already, red, blue and yellow, all mottled together.

'Why didn't you tell us? It looks hideous. You've obviously broken it.'

'What's the use?' Gareth said, in a dead voice. 'Nothing's any use is it, down here?'

A terrible empty feeling crept over Robert then. It was obvious that Gareth, who'd seemed the tough one, didn't really think they'd get out. This feeling was worse than panic, deeper than fear, and there was nothing beyond it, only the smell in the shaft, the darkness gathering above them, a sense of death.

Ten, twenty times he flung the rope out. At first it went nowhere near the mouth of the shaft but then he changed the way he was throwing, chucking it hard rather than unfolding it carefully, and it went higher like that. Twice the rope snaked up and hit the post, and once the loop opened up and held for a second before dropping down again.

'Why don't you let me have a go?' Gareth said quietly. 'I need to stand up, though.'

Robert moved over silently and helped him to his feet. 'Shine the flash-light on it, no, *there* . . .' the boy said tensely. Ping obeyed, trying to hold it steady.

His third throw caught the post and he tugged at the rope, pulling it over to the side of the shaft. They all stared up at it, not really believing their luck. 'All right,' Gareth said flatly, 'that's it. Who's going, then?'

Everything felt different then. Mentally they were out of the shaft and striding home across the moors. The two boys made a hand-hold for Ping to step into and then heaved her up as high as possible. She swung there for a minute in the soft darkness as the light from above dribbled away. In the silence they heard the knots squeak, and give a little, and the post bent slightly. But nothing broke.

She knew how to climb a rope because they did it in the gym at school, and she began to go up very slowly and methodically, looking down at the stained muddy faces below, then up to the circle of fading silver light. Already she could hear grass, she could smell sweet air. Robert would come up after her and they'd go and tell the Parrys, and bring help for Gareth. Her heart began to sing quietly. She, Ping, had saved them.

Then the shaft seemed to tumble and sway and become a hideous kaleidoscope. She was falling back again, bouncing and screaming, sprawled out again in the mud, with the rope in her hand. It was the rotten fence-post that had given, breaking beneath

145

her weight, lurching out of the crumbling earth and clattering down the shaft on top of her.

'It's all right, Ping,' Robert was saying, trying to get hold of her in the darkness. 'It's all *right*.' Gareth had passed out with the pain.

CHAPTER FIFTEEN

At one point Morgan and Idris were only yards away from the shaft, and if the three children had shouted loud enough they might well have heard them. But nobody was shouting now. Robert was slapping at Gareth's cheeks, trying to bring him round, and Ping was sobbing quietly, with her arms across her face.

'Come on,' Robert kept saying. 'We'll get out. Someone's bound to come in the end. We're OK.' But inside he felt helpless.

'I'm so cold,' she stammered. 'I'm absolutely freezing now. D'you think there's anything in his rucksack I could put on? He might have brought an extra jumper, or something.'

Robert opened the grubby canvas satchel. 'No, there's nothing. You could eat a bit of this chocolate. Don't suppose he'd mind.' Gareth was groaning, and once or twice he opened his eyes. 'We should give him a drink. There's a water-bottle here, or something.'

But the lump in the side-pocket was a screw-top bottle full of paraffin. Robert took the top off and sniffed at it. 'Wonder what he brought this for? It's full, too.' Then he remembered what the Parrys had told him, that the boy had come once to frighten them, and had set fire to the grass. He surely couldn't have been planning to slip away and leave them, while they were doing this walk? He looked at Gareth. His eyes were shut again, but he was still moaning. He'd told Robert all that was finished, that he'd tell somebody if Morgan made him go to the valley again, to put the frighteners on the Parrys. Perhaps the bottle was left over, forgotten, from a much earlier expedition. Was it though? He'd never get to the bottom of Gareth Morgan.

He dug down into the pouch again and found a match-box, then he looked at the bottle of paraffin, and at the rag prison rope, and an idea came to him.

At first the men had shouted, Morgan barking out angry cries, Preece halloing and whistling in his thin voice. And they'd listened carefully for some kind of answer, flashing their torches round the dark hills.

Idris had been pulling his boots on in Aunt Em's kitchen when Reg Morgan had appeared in the doorway, with mud all over him, in a filthy tweed coat. He'd not bothered to explain anything. 'I know which route they took,' he'd said. 'Gareth left me a note. Always has to do that,' he added, 'when he takes himself off anywhere. I reckon they must have lost the track and gone up above the valleys. Where's the boy's father?'

'They phoned from the hospital this afternoon. He's still up there,' Dilys said. Morgan just grunted. 'Can't you get him back?' he said. 'We might need three. He ought to know.'

'The baby's on its way. I'm not worrying him yet, Reg. You go with Idris. They'll be all right, they're sensible kids,' she said calmly.

But Morgan didn't seem convinced. 'I've got a rope,' he said as they left the cottage, 'and some whisky.'

Idris could smell it. He reckoned Reg Morgan must have had quite a few already, but he said nothing. He'd known the man all his life: even before they were in the infants at the village school they'd played together. He'd always been a bit of a bully, a bit of a swaggerer; money had made him worse. It was his wife dying that had really changed him though. Eileen Morgan was sweet, Dilys's best friend. Everyone said it was the best thing that had happened to Reg Morgan, that he was different when he was with her. Then she'd died in their kitchen, making the tea. Even now he only said she'd *gone*, as if she'd just walked out one day, and left him. He still couldn't use the word 'death'.

As they walked, Reg Morgan was thinking of all the times he'd been over these hills when he was a younger man, and as a boy before that. He remembered the shafts on the slopes of Moel-y-bryn, and going down the smaller ones on ropes, for a dare. He'd done that with Idris Preece, one summer.

But Idris was a town man now. He worked in a factory in Llandewi, he wouldn't be able to locate those shafts, not in the dark. And memory was playing strange tricks on Morgan too. He thought the really big holes had been higher up, on the first ridge of the mountain. They laboured up it steadily now, in silence, walking further and further away from the children, under the low hump of Moel-y-bryn.

'Will it work?' Ping whispered, helping Robert spread the rope out over the map, to save it from the mud. 'I can't see how.'

'There's a chance. Hope the matches aren't damp. We've got to try something.'

'They may be, they've been there for weeks,' Gareth said defensively. 'So's the paraffin.' His voice was weak but at least he'd come round again.

Robert picked out a stone from the side of the shaft with his penknife and knotted one end of the rope round it, then he rolled the whole thing up into a ball. The rags were soaked in the paraffin, they'd used every drop of it.

'Can you give me a leg up, Ping? Use your hands.'

She staggered slightly as he stepped in the palm-hold she had made for him. 'Lean against the wall – that's it. *Now*.'

He couldn't throw as hard as Gareth but all he had to do was get the stone out of the hole, and onto the dry grass. He lobbed it half a dozen times, almost blindly in the yellow fading light from the torch, then at last it didn't come back. 'That's it,' he muttered, his heart thudding. 'It's gone somewhere anyhow. Brace yourself, Ping, I've almost lost this end.' He jumped up and grabbed, then fell down on top of her, accidentally kicking the side of Gareth's head as he came down. Neither of them even spoke. Gareth just rubbed the mud away and Ping tried to straighten up. They were all filthy, wet and stinking, and feeling cold. A deadness had come over them now, and they couldn't smell the rotting sheep any more, or recognise the hunger cramps slicing through them.

There were only three matches in the box and the first two went out immediately. 'They're damp Gareth, I can't risk the third.'

'Use the map then, use it as a spill. See if there's any paraffin left first, to make it go.'

Ping shook a few last drops out of the bottle on to the twisted paper torch and Robert moved over by Gareth, to where the rag rope dangled, feet above his head. 'Light the match, Ping. Don't drop it for God's sake, then I'll get the rope going.'

The match fizzled and went out almost at once, but the screwed-up map had taken hold and it flared up. Robert dabbed repeatedly at the soaked rope until his fingers were burning, then he dropped the flaming paper and Ping trampled it in the mud at the bottom of the hole. For a second they had been warm, and in the light. Now the dark slumped over them again, like a great mouth.

But a small flame was creeping fitfully up the side of the shaft, like mercury in a thermometer. They watched, sick with expectation. What if they'd missed a bit and it died out? There'd not been so much paraffin, not for all that material, and it had been muddy and damp. But the flame was still travelling and now, after what felt like centuries, they watched it reach the rim of the shaft.

Robert's nerves gave way suddenly and he closed his eyes. They'd been mad to try this, they could turn the hole into a raging inferno, there might be explosive gases. He started to shake, and a scream rose inside him.

Then there was a muffled explosion, quite far-off, and muted, like the popping of a gas-ring but louder, and when he opened his eyes he saw that the shaft was ringed with fire, and he could hear the dry grass crackling.

Dan Parry had been out looking for them too. He'd heard in the tiny hamlet, at the bottom of their track, that three children were missing out on the moors, and that the police were coming from Denbigh. He'd been waiting for Robert and his sister anyway, waiting in the hut with his father, with the ring on the table. Four o'clock the boy had said . . . half past four, at the very latest. Then, when nobody came, he'd had a walk down to Rowlands' place, near the road. It was Dai Rowland who'd told him. He'd built the fire up for the old man and set off with a rope round his waist, and an old blanket. He didn't need maps.

He was at the valley head, in the darkness, wondering whether to go back to his father, then down to see if Dai had any news, when the night turned to fire below him, away over the moor. And he heard voices. With the rope trailing off his waist and the torn blanket flapping, he ran like a maniac towards the blaze. A patch of grass in the shadow of Moel-y-bryn was burning, and the broken fence-posts speared the dancing light, pointing the way to the shaft. He stopped only to stamp the grass out, beating at it with the blanket till the flames hissed and died, then he was on his knees, shouting their names and unwinding his rope. When Morgan and Idris got there Robert was already out of the hole, and they were pulling Ping up.

The two Elliott children were soon muffled in blankets and Jim Preece was giving them something from a flask. Morgan just stood over the hole, limp and helpless, while things went on round him. He kept saying 'He's dead, isn't he? I know he's dead.'

'Oh hush, man,' Dan Parry said, through his back. 'We'll get him out.'

'Why doesn't he speak to us?'

'He keeps fainting. It's his ankle,' Robert said. 'He crushed it when we fell. We didn't know what to do.'

They knotted one rope into a harness and Dan climbed down with it. Very gently and carefully he pulled and pushed at Gareth till he was fastened into it, like a chair; then they slowly pulled him to the top of the shaft, letting the rope down again for Dan. When the cool night air hit his face Gareth opened his eyes and tried to stand. Then he saw his father.

The big man swayed slightly and took a step towards him. Gareth tottered and fell forwards and Morgan put his arms round him, burying his fat red face in the dark matted hair. Nobody else moved but the night was full of sounds, Robert and Ping warming up in their blankets, Dan Parry coiling his ropes, Idris at a loss, rubbing Morgan's silver hip-flask to a shine on his boilersuit.

And the man seemed unable to let Gareth go. But in the end he helped him to sit down on the grass and bound the ankle up with rags. Dan stood over them as he did it, an untidy black silhouette turning grey, as the dawn began. Morgan stood up at last, opened his mouth suddenly then slowly shut it again. Then he took hold of Dan Parry's hand and held it for a long time.

Dad didn't come back to the cottage till late in the afternoon of the next day. He'd been with Mum all that time, and they'd not told him about the three children falling down the shaft. Then he rang Dilys and said he was coming home. In a panic she got the children up, shaking them awake out of their ten hours' sleep, and helping them to get dressed.

He looked very white and tired. Dilys told him about the accident, but it didn't seem to register, he just hugged them silently. Both the children felt as if they were only half in this world. There was a bandage round Ping's head and they both had bruised faces,

153

but their father still didn't ask them what had happened. He wasn't really there either. He was still in the hospital, with Mum.

When he came into the big room and flopped down in a chair, Dilys disappeared and shut the door. Nick had crept in and climbed onto his knee.

'I've got some news,' he told them. 'You've got a baby sister. She arrived a few weeks early, at five o'clock this afernoon, and she's rather small. She's beautiful though. She looks just like Ping.'

'But how's Mum?' they all said together. Babies were boring at first. They wanted to know about Mum.

'She's well, oh she's wonderfully well. She wants you all to come and see her, first thing this evening.'

There were tears in his eyes. Nick said shrilly, 'You're crying, Daddy. Why? Don't have that sad face.' He reached up and put his hands round his father's neck.

'It's OK, Nick,' Dad said, in a sort of strangled whisper. 'Grown-ups are daft really. They cry sometimes because they're happy, don't they, Robert?'

He caught at his son's fingers, and held them. Robert could only nod. He felt so tired and relieved and mixed-up. He was crying too.

CHAPTER SIXTEEN

Midnight, and he was in the dark again, on his own.
Up till now he'd only been alone at Aunt Em's during
the day. At nights someone else had always been
there, and there were all the reassuring sounds you
listened for in bed, cisterns gurgling and pipes click-
ing. There was an uncanny quietness in the house
tonight, and nobody in the cottage except him, staring
at the bedroom wall with his torch in his hand.

It was four weeks since they'd been rescued from
the shaft and Dad still hadn't raged at them. Robert
wondered if it had all been made light of by Dilys, and
whether he knew what had actually happened. When
Mum asked about the bruises, and Ping's bandage,
they'd told her the den had collapsed with them all in
it. It was an official lie, sanctioned by Dad, who didn't
want her worrying. When they were home again, he
said, they could tell her everything. He hardly
mentioned their fall into the shaft, he seemed much
too worried about the new-baby, and what was
happening at Steeles.

Mum was still in hospital because after the first few
days things had started to go wrong. The baby
couldn't feed properly so they'd had to give it in-
jections and run a lot of tests. Mum looked weary and

hollow-eyed these days and when they went to see her she just lay back listlessly on the pillows and listened to them all blathering on. Dad tore about in his car, going from the hospital back to Buckden Heath, then sometimes to Aunt Em's for an hour with them, then back to Steeles. He never seemed to eat or sleep or sit down, and everyone was getting bad-tempered. It seemed so long since they had all been together.

Then, marvellously, things had begun to come right. Two days ago the baby had at last started to gain weight, and they were slowly cutting out all the special treatment. Mum could have it in the room with her now, and she looked a lot happier. There was even talk of letting her come home at the end of next week. Dad had brought Grandma to see the baby for the first time and he was spending the night with her near Chester. Ping and Nick were sleeping at Dilys's for a 'treat'. Robert himself was supposed to be up at Morgans', keeping Gareth company.

His ankle had set wrongly and they'd had to break it and start again, otherwise they said he might limp for ever. He was wobbling about on crutches now with a great plaster cast on. Ping had done funny drawings all over it with felt-tipped pens.

Morgan was fussing over Gareth. A television set had appeared and been installed in the farm kitchen where he had to spend a lot of the time on the settee, with his leg up. Then he came back from Llandewi library with a pile of books, and he'd also been to the best men's outfitters in the town, to get him new clothes, socks, sweaters, jeans and boots. It must have cost a small fortune.

Reg Morgan found speech hard. When he spoke to anyone, Gareth included, he seemed to spit the words out, like stones. So he just kept on giving things, like the puppy, and the clothes, and the TV set.

Robert didn't doubt now that he cared for Gareth very much in his own twisted kind of way. That night on the mountain his face had been distorted with pain, with the sheer anguish of his imaginings about the one son that was left to him, and about what might have happened to him, down the shaft. He'd become childish. 'He's dead, I know he's dead' was all he could say and he'd been no use to anyone. It was Idris and Dan who'd done all the practical things.

One morning he'd turned up in Aunt Em's kitchen and muttered something about the puppy, something like 'Dog's growing fast, needs a breather. Driving him mad, being shut up all day. Worth a packet too.' Robert tried not to think of Rags, the ugly pathetic other dog who'd not been worth a penny. He agreed to go up and exercise Jem any time, and to stay the night with Gareth now and then, if he wanted company. He felt sorry for him, stuck in that farmhouse all day; the accident in the shaft had brought them closer together.

Gareth still had his moods. Sometimes, when Robert went to see him, he hardly squeezed three sentences out; on those days he obviously didn't want any company, apart from Jem's. But now and again they had really good talks. He knew a lot about farming and animals, even though he was determined not to take over from his father; he knew a lot about this part of Wales too, and quite a bit about the ancient Parry family. They'd done the border fights at school too, but he'd not told Robert till now.

He seemed to need much longer to warm up than most people. 'Give him time' Mum had advised

Robert, from her hospital bed, when he complained about the moodiness. She liked Gareth a lot and now he was laid up himself, with his ankle, they wrote little letters to each other. Waiting for her at home, on top of the piano, was his father's old record, the one he'd loved but wouldn't listen to anymore. 'What is life for me without thee? What is life if thou art dead?'

Tonight Dilys thought he'd arranged to go to Morgans'; Dad thought they were all at Dilys's; Gareth thought he was there, too. Nobody knew he'd stayed behind at Aunt Em's, waiting for the darkness. It was rather sly of him, but it might be the only chance he'd ever have. Aunt Em had written to tell them that the cottage was being put up for sale within the next few months. There was no talk of her coming back from New Zealand. When Mum came out of hospital with the baby the Elliotts would be going straight back to Buckden Heath.

In the same post as Aunt Em's letter there'd been a fat one for him, redirected from the cottage by Dilys. A printed label in the corner told him it was from Hugo Powell. He tore upstairs and shut himself in his attic, to read it in peace.

In flowery, almost illegible handwriting the composer thanked them for their letter and said he would by no means rule out their theory about a link between Aunt Em's cottage and the Parry family. Rachel's story was a tragic one. Indeed, it had led him to write what many people had regarded as his finest piece of music so far. If they did discover anything, he would be very interested to hear. For now, he enclosed a photocopy of the relevant story from *Clwyd Legends*. He was sorry it was rather faint.

Robert had pored over the stapled sheets, and when

Ping came back from a piano lesson, and climbed the attic stairs to find him, he was sitting on his bed still staring at them. 'Read this,' he said, thrusting the photocopies into her hand. 'I can hardly believe it, really. But we're *right* about the cottage. I'm sure we're right.'

According to the author of *Clwyd Legends* Rachel Parry had been the daughter of yet another Daniel, an early 19th century one this time, a wealthy landowner who had lost his wife (in childbirth) and his two sons in the Napoleonic Wars. Rachel, the youngest child by several years, was all that remained to him and his devotion to her was legendary. *As the years went by*, the author had written, *and the old man's wounds slowly began to heal, and become part of him, his feeling for this daughter, the child of his old age, blossomed at last like a great tree.*

Rachel, the fountain of his loneliness and sorrow, became his greatest comfort, his bright hope, and when rich men looked at her, and murmured of estates and dowries, he would not listen to them. She could not leave him yet. He was old now and he prayed that the Lord would take him while she was still in his house.

The sad, simple tale was all couched in this rather flowery language. Robert would have been impatient with it in any other circumstances but he knew he had to read every word. As he did so, his excitement slowly mounted.

These Parrys had apparently lived through very hard times, through a kind of 19th century 'slump' that had followed the end of the wars in Europe, times when food was scarce and work almost impossible to find. The now penniless farmers were burning down all the toll gates rather than pay greedy landowners precious coin to go through, with their flocks. As they did so they shouted 'The seed of Rebecca shall destroy the gates of her enemies.' A little footnote explained that these violent incidents had gone down in Welsh history as 'the Rebecca riots'.

The ageing Daniel Parry, the story continued, while continuing to live in comfort *on a windy hill somewhere above the hamlet of Groeyurgoch, behaved generously through those years of want. Ancient family treasures were sent to London to be sold, and mysterious gifts made to the people that all knew must have come from him. On his many farms and small-holdings he took on more and more labourers, while others got rid of the few they had.*

But it was not enough. Had he sold everything he possessed he might have been spared. But he had his dignity. He continued to live in his comfortable house on the hill and Rachel wore silk dresses, and they ate meat and white milk-bread.

It was another great family, with whom the Parrys had warred centuries ago, that brought him down. 'What a man soweth that also shall he reap.' These men, unlike the philanthropic Daniel Parry, had dealt harshly with those who had served them and now they were in want themselves.

One night, in late summer, when there had been a few quiet months, and no trouble from the mobs in the Llandewi valley, the old man was coming home late, from business in Denbigh. He was anxious as he rode home. It was already dark, and his daughter was alone.

As he turned his horse into the rutted lane that climbed up the steep hill to the house, four horsemen clattered past in the gloom. He could just make out their faces, and he knew them all. They were the four sons of that rival family which had fallen on hard times, in the famine years. It was they who were causing the troubles in the valley, going round to inflame the hungry people, herding them into mobs, and leading them out on their desperate, scavenging journeys. A dread clawed at him, and he kicked the lumbering horse to go quicker, up the hill.

The house was ringed by trees, and dark, but he could smell the burning and hear the crackle and hiss of flame as the nearer branches caught fire. Mad with fear for his daughter he stood in the doorway, calling her name, but even as he wrapped his cloak about his head the main timbers fell in, turning everything into a sheet of flame.

He stumbled helplessly away, driven back by the immense heat. The burning house illuminated the countryside and he could see up the fields to the dark barren moors beyond, and to the darker mountains. Something was lying in a heap, out on the grass, something like a swirl of red silk, a thing darker than the leaping flames, more the colour of blood.

They had fired a shot at his daughter as she tried to get away from them, away on to the moors where she could hide till her father came back. A single shot, in the back of the head, and the pistol lay beside her, warm from the flames.

By the time the villagers saw the fire and began to climb the hill a wild rain was falling. It had been a close muggy day, with grumblings of thunder over the mountains. Now, as Daniel Parry stood over his daughter's body, the raging house behind him, the black moors beyond, lightning ripped the sky open and one massive thunderbolt brought the storm.

By dawn the house stood blackened and roofless, eaten away from its broad perimeter by the great jaws of the fire. Only the heart of it still stood against the sky, the clutch of tiny thick-walled rooms that had been the ancient beginnings of Daniel Parry's great house.

Of the old man himself there was no sign. They crowded in from the villages, kinsmen and friends, nameless folk he had been kind to. But he was never seen in that valley again.

He ended his days in another valley, far from those who had known him, where there was a small summer dwelling tenanted for him by a young cousin, in the summer months. He must have walked all night, with the dead girl in his arms, walked blindly on over the storm-blown moorlands, driven on by rage, and grief, and hopelessness. And on that valley floor he laboured and prepared another fire. It was gigantic. It was a funeral pyre for his daughter Rachel, and when it was well alight he consigned her body to the flames, in the ancient manner of the gypsy people, like the outcast he now was.

From sunrise till dusk the fire burned steadily, and those who heard of it, who had cared for him and searched for him in vain, made their way to the secret place. They brought food for him, clothing and money. They lined the valley ridge with their pitying faces, staring silently down at the sight in the bottom of the canyon, the fantastic fire, the heap of gifts beside it, the old man standing there like stone, his white hair streaming out in the wind, the tears on his face.

He lived in the valley, with his cousin, until he died, but he survived only for a few months, after his daughter's death, for with Rachel gone there was nothing left in the world for him, and it was time to die. His killers, too, were dead before the year was out. The four wild sons of Roland Morgan were hunted down and shot, and many would have done it, for the Morgan family, whose feud with the Parrys in ancient times had passed into history, were hated now.

So ended the story of Daniel Parry and his daughter Rachel, and with it the story of two great families, the Parrys and the Morgans. And on the rough stone that marked the grave of the four brothers was inscribed a hard truth: 'Vengeance is mine, I will repay, sayeth the Lord.'

Robert wasn't a dreamer, his size 11 shoes were firmly planted on the ground. He didn't have Ping's wild imagination, and music didn't do for him what it did for his mother, or for Gareth Morgan. He was the strictly practical member of the family, some might say 'thick'. But when he thought of that wall in his room he was a changed person. Something like madness possessed him then. When he thought of the Parrys, and the night of the burning, all the years of history seemed to beat down upon him like tremendous rain, relentlessly, driving him on.

Mum and Dad had spent ages arguing over names for the new baby, and for weeks she'd been called 'It', alternating with 'Boris'. Then, at last, they'd settled on 'Rachel', Grandma Elliott's second name. (Her first was 'Lilian' but she'd never liked that).

When Dad told them Robert hadn't said anything, but his ears had made a strange singing noise. So there was to be a second Rachel in the old cottage, a tiny modern one, a pink squealing white-wrapped bundle in a hospital cot, ages removed from her graver nineteenth century sister who had stumbled away from the burning house, away up the fields to her own death. It was a sign to him. He had to break through, and on his own. Ping would be hurt when she found out, especially since she'd read the story too, but he couldn't help it. For this he couldn't have anyone with him.

First he hammered a blanket over the window, otherwise light would pass straight through the thin curtains and shine on to the road. Someone coming home might see, and Dilys would get to hear about it, and come up to investigate. Then he got his tools ready. In the barn he'd found a big square hammer, the kind they used in quarries. He would use this to swing at the wall, from a distance, but first he must pick the plaster off.

For this he used his small hammer and chisel. The new cement was spread thinly and he soon got it off, and pushed it in a damp heap in the corner of the room. The first layer of stones was now exposed and he was able to loosen the boulder he and Gareth had got out, which his father had cemented back roughly. He staggered when the weight of it dropped into his hands, and it fell through his fingers and crashed down on to the floor.

The noise was like a small explosion in the still house. Half of him waited for lights to go on everywhere, for footsteps to come pounding up the uncarpeted stairs, but the old cottage slumbered on. Even now, unpeopled and cold, it felt like home. When he thought of Aunt Em, selling it and that they could never come to it again, his heart ached.

He swung his hammer wildly at the wall but nothing much happened. A few chips of stone fluttered down and drifted about on the floor. Then he tried again but it was hard work because he couldn't seem to balance the tool properly so that the full force would smash against the wall. In the end he put it to one side and took up the chisel and his small hammer. He'd just have to take the boulders out one by one.

He stood back and surveyed the wall. They were more or less in rows. To make a space big enough to get through he'd need three boulders out of the first row and the same three in the row underneath. It was going to take a long time. But he could see the second wall in the space where the first stone had gone. It might just be thinner. Old as he was, Daniel Parry must have worked fast, walling up his secret in a few hours, frightened in case the Morgans came back, with their guns and knives. Robert set to work.

When he looked at his watch again it was half past two and six stones were at his feet, in a small cairn. His hands were raw and bleeding and he felt very cold. They were well into August and the trees outside already had that dead end-of-summer look. There was an autumn chill about, and the old house smelt of September.

He found another jumper in his chest of drawers and pulled it on, looking at the wall as he did so. Behind the boulders was a whitish-brown surface, speckled darkly with bits of gravel. It looked like builder's rubble mixed with sweepings from a path. Were there more great stones behind it? It was hard to believe that one old man could have done all this, working in the dark, with the threat of murderers at his back. He would know soon.

He knocked gently at the knobbly wall with his bloody knuckles, listening carefully. It sounded thinner. So he pushed against it, sideways, and he thought, though only fractionally, a millionth of an inch, that something gave way.

He swung the big hammer like an axe now, and the rubble disintegrated, showering about like white feathers. His heart began pounding. Tension, panic and hope gave enormous strength to his thin arms and he swung the hammer higher and higher. In the small room the noise was unbearably loud, crashing inside his head like an enormous gong. Sparks flew as the metal hit something in the wall and bounced off the floor, like red rain from a firework.

Then he misjudged and swung the hammer too high. There was a crash and glass rained down on him, slicing into his cheek. He'd hit the light bulb, and now he was in the dark, but he couldn't stop the fall of the hammer. It was his biggest blow yet and as he stood there blindly the head crashed home.

There was a rumble and a rolling about of stones, and the room filled with dust. Then he heard a pattering, like scree trickling down the side of a mountain. Then silence. He stood quite still, feeling behind him for the torch that lay on his bed. His shaking fingers closed on it at last and he flashed it at the wall. The inner layer had given way in a lump and there was a gash of darkness. Dust swirled about him in thick grey plumes and there was a strange smell, a bit like overripe apples.

He went right up to the hole. The bottom of it was level with his chest and it was just big enough to climb through. Slowly he shone his torch-beam into the blackness. At first he could see nothing, then he started back in terror. The yellow line of light had caught something, some large and glittering thing that was looking straight at him. It was an eye.

He wanted to run away, to tear down the hill to Dilys's cottage, to confess, and be tucked up in a warm bed. But he didn't move. Fear washed over him, then ebbed away, and he felt icy calm. How could it be an *eye*? It must be a bit of glass or metal, caught in the torch-light. He flashed the beam in again but it was still there, gleaming, a big oval of clear amber.

He put the torch between his teeth, clutched at the rim of the hole and pulled himself up. His mind was white and empty. All he could think of was something he'd whispered to Ping when she was so frightened in the shaft. 'Come on girl,' he'd said. 'Be brave. Don't cry. Remember, we're on the lion's side.' Her lion, in that fairy story she liked so much, the lion that stood for courage and strength. He'd laughed at her once, but he needed that courage now.

He dropped down into the hole, flashing his torch about, and saw ancient floor-boards, fitted together with wooden pegs, with grey-black markings over the swirl of the wood. Some of them were charred and the grey plaster walls were plumed with dark streamers. He actually thought he could still smell smoke.

The space he was standing in was as wide as his bedroom and went back about five feet. It felt strangely warm. He worked out that he was just over the Aga cooker which was fixed in the middle of a massive double wall. That wall, and the space above it, were all that were left of Daniel Parry's house, the most ancient part that the fire had not consumed, the 'clutch' of tiny rooms described in *Clwyd Legends*. There must have been enough of the stone stairway left for the old man to climb up, enough floor intact for him to labour on, into the night hours, and build the wall, and disappear. A note in the Rachel Parry photocopy said the ruin had been shunned for many months, after the young girl's murder.

At last, his hands shaking with nerves, he shone the torch at the thing with the eye. It was huge and black and when he touched it, it moved gently, crunching back and forth over the rubble on the floor. It was a rocking horse, a great black stallion on wide bow-shaped rockers, the ends curled round like the capitals of Ionic pillars. Its tail had disintegrated, the ribbons of its mane fell to dust as it moved, but its eyes were bright glass in the torch-light, and its mouth still flared open in triumph.

Then he noticed that things were heaped all round the rockers, and he saw a tiny child's chair with a seat

167

of curly elm and smooth beech-wood arms, with three dolls on it. Their clothes had disintegrated and the stuffed arms and legs had rotted away to shapeless lumps. But their faces remained, pink and white porcelain, with rosebud lips and tiny noses, the cheeks framed in tiny curls.

There were the kind of toys he'd only seen in museums, a whip and a top, wooden animals on wheels, a cup and ball carved with ivy leaves, bone dice and big painted playing cards, a set of ivory five-stones. Books were piled everywhere but he couldn't read the titles in the wobbling light.

When he stood up and looked at the walls he saw a picture on a nail behind the rocking horse. It was a sampler, a needlework picture for little girls to practise their stitches. He read the spidery letters with difficulty, holding the torch up:

> When wealth to virtuous hand is given
> It blesses like the dews of heaven,
> Like Heaven it hears the orphans' cries
> And wipes the tears from widows' eyes.

The stitching underneath read 'Rachel Parry hic fecit, April 19th 1824, in the eighth year of her age.' Then there was some Welsh writing, the letters of the alphabet, and the numbers one to ten.

This was her room, or part of it, the nursery where she'd played on the rocking horse and set out her dolls, the place she'd retired to when she was older, in a silk dress and with her hair up, to sew or read the calf-covered books, to pore over her father's house-hold accounts, now she was becoming a woman, somebody the old man could lean on.

The place he stood in was a memorial to Rachel. The old man, crazed by grief and loss, had crept back from his secret valley at night to the abandoned house, and reverently put together all that had been hers, the books, the toys, the dolls in their frilled dresses, all the pathetic apparatus of childish days.

Then he had built a wall against intruders and against prying eyes, sealing away all that was left of her, just as his own memories were sealed now, in his heart, beyond the grasp of men, precious, untouchable.

Robert looked again at the heap on the floor and didn't want to be there. He was an intruder also.

He shone the torch one last time round the small smoke-blackened space and the beam caught something new. Carefully he crept round the rocking-horse to the far corner of the room, to where a small object was standing on the floor, on its own. He knelt down and touched it. It was hard, and very cold.

Robert rubbed at it with his sleeve, then looked again. The gleam was gold. It was a small urn, a sister to the 'funerary' urns in the museum, with the same lion head carved on it. The pale metal still shone after so many winters entombed in this secret place, this sanctuary, that had coffined up in silence for more than a century an old father's pain and grief.

He didn't need to put his hand inside, for he knew what it must contain. Ashes, soft and grey, the colour of pigeons, wood ashes from a great fire, mingled, he was certain, with the ashes of a young girl who had died so pointlessly out there on the hillside, all those years ago.

CHAPTER SEVENTEEN

It was Saturday morning in Church Stoken. The car joined a long traffic jam on the edge of the village, getting slower and slower, then stopped completely. 'This is terrible,' Dad grumbled, winding the window down and looking out, 'the queue's half a mile long. We'll be here all day.'

'Why didn't we come last night?' Nick said.

'I told you, we *couldn't*.'

'Aren't the trees lovely?' Mum said calmly, looking at the orchards on her side of the road, and she held Rachel up to see the glory of pink and white blossom.

Robert looked at his sister's round moon-face. She really was much too fat. It was hard to believe that this was the scraggy creature he'd seen in an incubator, only seven months ago. 'Making up for lost time,' Mum said defensively if anyone suggested she was overweight.

Nick was on the lion's side and he'd been waiting for the car to come level with the chapel. Suddenly he shrieked 'The lion's gone!' It was true. The plinth the statue had rested on showed only the palest outline of a crouching animal, and behind it, on the wall, was a notice in big red letters: 'Folk Museum Here. Official opening July 1st.'

'They must have put it inside, for safety's sake,' Dad said. 'I'm surprised they didn't do it years ago. It might be quite interesting to have a look round, when they open up.'

Nick was badgering his father to stop so they could go and find the lion but Mr Elliott wasn't listening. He was staring straight ahead at the traffic jam, tapping his fingers on the steering wheel, preoccupied and tense.

'They should build a by-pass round this place,' he was muttering. 'It'd make life a lot easier.'

What does it matter now? Robert was thinking. We won't be making this journey any more.

So the lion had gone from the side of the road; it was the landmark they always looked for when they were going to Aunt Em's. A chill crept over him as he stared at the empty space. Nothing had actually been *said* but he knew what this journey was for. They were going to the cottage to say goodbye.

He'd not really felt like a hero but he was surprised at the numbers of people who kept phoning them up, about his discovery. The police and the people from the Museum of Wales had been very discreet but the news still got out surprisingly quickly. It was inevitable in a small gossipy place like Groeyurgoch.

Newspaper men had kept driving up to the cottage and asking him for an 'exclusive'. He described what had happened, as precisely as he could, but the articles they wrote were ridiculous. 'Schoolboy stumbles on robber's hoard' was one headline. 'Probably the most significant find since Tutenkhamen's tomb' another read. That was pushing it, but at least it didn't imply that Daniel Parry had been a kind of thief. Robert had appeared on BBC Wales for five minutes, to tell the viewers what had happened. It had been interesting going to a television studio, and he got a few letters afterwards from people who'd seen him. After that the interest had fizzled out remarkably quickly.

It was probably a good thing, too, because Ping was getting rather jealous. Every time the telephone rang it had been somebody wanting to talk to Robert. His parents were very calm about it all, except for his father's anxiety about Aunt Em's property. For safety the hole had been widened into a small archway by a builder, and given brick supports at either side. For the moment nothing else could be done about it, not till Aunt Em came back.

Mum had kept all the newspaper articles, with Robert peering out at the world underneath fat black capitals. 'You're a strange boy,' was all Dad had said, looking at them. 'And a disobedient one. I knew you were up to something.' But he smiled at him as he said it.

Robert's last memory of Aunt Em's was standing in the doorway of his bedroom watching the museum people at work. Every single thing he'd found had to be labelled, numbered, and put into packing cases. The men worked slowly, meticulously, with hushed voices. The room felt full of reverence for old things. That was right, Robert thought. It had been Rachel Parry's room.

The sale of the cottage had been held up because of what Robert had found, but it had been impossible to get there for weeks anyway. It was a harsh December and a worse January and there were terrible fogs. Robert had sat over the gas-fire in his attic bedroom, looking out over the dark town, thinking of Gareth and his dad and Jem, thinking of the Parrys, wanting to be there.

Nothing he'd found was likely to be of great value, except the urn, and it would be months before any decision was made about that. It had to be examined, photographed, dated and valued, then the legal position would be discussed, or so Dad told them. If the rightful owners could be tracked down everything would go to their surviving family. Only if nobody could be proved to have a claim on it would the finder, Robert, get anything.

'I bet Aunt Em'll get it,' Ping announced as the car plunged into the familiar lanes near Groeyurgoch. 'That's what always happens. Things never go to people who need them, like the Parrys, and I bet it's theirs, really.'

'They'll be all right now, whatever happens,' Mum said. 'All they wanted was to stay where they were, and they can. Gareth's father's been helping them do their place up, so Mrs Preece told me; well he sent a couple of his men over.'

Robert hadn't heard about that, but it fitted. Reg Morgan would never get in his car and drive along the rutted track to see the Parrys himself, he'd just look after them through other people, send them things. That would be his way of saying he wanted there to be peace between them, perhaps, and that he was sorry. Another interpretation was that he had a guilty conscience. Well, whatever his thinking, it was better than nothing, a whole lot better. It made the last trip to Aunt Em's less bitter somehow.

It was *their* family that really needed the money. Steeles had got rid of two more people since Fred, and

Dad said it was his turn next. They were finishing a big project, a sports centre for the paper factory in Buckden, and after that, Dad had confided to him, there was nothing left for him to do. The work they'd have then didn't need three architects. He'd been looking round for another job, but nothing had turned up yet.

There'd been no mention of going to Aunt Em's till the Thursday night, then Dad had asked Robert if he had to play football at school, on the Saturday.

'There's no match this week. Why?'

'I was going to ask you if you could get out of it. We've got to go to the cottage.'

'Why?'

'Oh, you know, clear things up a bit.' His voice was a bit peculiar.

'Is Aunt Em back, then?'

'No, but she phoned us. From New Zealand.'

'From *New Zealand*?' Ping repeated. 'Has she got the money for those things already then?'

Mum had opened her mouth to say something, then shut it again reluctantly. But there was something special in the way she looked at the three children, a sort of calm cheerfulness, and Robert saw her exchange one of her smiles with Dad. Then he heard his father humming as he went up the stairs. He'd not done that for months.

They went to the cottage the longer way round, through the village, and saw two notices. Both announced the sale, by auction, of Aunt Em's cottage. 'March 27th' Ping read stonily. 'That's next Saturday.'

'D'you suppose my find'll make any difference?' Robert said. 'Will more people come?'

'Bound to,' Dad said. 'People are very nosy, and it

was in all the papers. They often go to auctions with no intention of buying anything. Still, this isn't a sale of the contents, it's only a house after all.'

Only a house. He'd thought that a year ago, when they'd first seen the cottage, when his father had been so excited by it. He'd not understood, not then.

'They've banged a notice in, right on the verge,' Ping snorted. 'Look how they've squashed the daffodils.' The poster was like the others they'd seen in the village, red and black. 'For Sale by Auction, March 27th.' But across it was pasted a diagonal strip. 'WITHDRAWN'.

Nick was already out of the car and running across the paddock to his den. Dad unlocked the kitchen door and was pushing it open.

'The Aga's on. That's good. And Dilys has left us a loaf, and some milk. She is *good*.' It was like the first time.

'I don't understand,' Robert said. 'What does "Withdrawn" mean?'

'There isn't going to be an auction. Aunt Em's changed her mind.'

Mum's voice was a bit trembly. She pulled a stool out from under the kitchen table, and sat down on it, with Rachel on her lap.

Robert and Ping thought she was going to cry.

'We're buying it,' Dad said, and sat down suddenly too, putting his arm round Mum. His voice was quiet, but his big, calm face had suddenly changed, as if, inside him, somebody had switched a light on. He looked happier, and more relaxed, than he had been for over a year.

For a minute nobody spoke, then Ping said anxiously 'But how *can* we live here? What about our house in Buckden? And what about going to work?'

'I'm leaving Steeles,' Dad said. 'It's as simple as that.'

'But Dad, what about a job?' Robert whispered, not daring to believe any of it.

'I'm setting up on my own, in Llandewi – well, with Fred, actually. He did get some money from Steeles, after a lot of hassle. We're using that, and borrowing some more. We'll be partners.'

'Is there enough work, though?'

'Enough to keep us going for a bit, and there's a promise of more. It's what I've always wanted. If I don't do it now I never will. You've got to take risks sometimes.'

'I know.'

'But what about Aunt Em?'

'Well, you can stop calling her Aunt Meanie, for a start,' Dad said. 'We've got to sell our own house, before we can buy this place off her, and I don't suppose it'll go in five minutes. But she'll wait. She says she's quite happy to. And in view of the fact that Robert actually tried to knock it *down* –'

'She really didn't want it to go out of her family, you know,' Mum said. 'I think that helped to persuade her, though she'd have got much more at an auction.'

'But why didn't you tell us *before*?' Robert asked. There was a queer tight feeling in his throat now.

'We couldn't,' Dad said. 'I didn't dare, in case it all fell through. I only got the final details sorted out with Fred on Tuesday, then we had to speak to Aunt Em again, and the solicitors. Anyway,' he added with a grin, 'I'd have thought you'd have understood a little deception, you of all people.'

Nick was standing in the doorway, listening. He'd

heard the bits about changing jobs, and having no money. 'Will there be enough to *eat*?' he said, trying to climb on to Mum's knee, and dislodging Rachel, who started to cry. 'And can I have those new sneakers?'

'Oh, we'll survive,' Dad said, grabbing the baby and hoisting her into the air, till she squealed with delight. 'It'll be quite a different sort of life here though, dull and quiet, two buses a week, bad weather, stuck up here on this hill, day in, day out. Can you bear it, Ping?'

She didn't answer at first but a familiar dreamy expression was creeping slowly across her face. 'Well,' she said at last, 'I hope I'll get to know people, when I go to a new school, and . . . and I've always loved Aunt Em's. Yes, I think I can bear it, Dad,' and she hugged him.

'Where are you off to?' he said, as Robert slid out of the door.

'Well, I thought I'd just run up and tell Gareth.'

It was almost a year since they'd first slept at the cottage. This morning he'd thought they were leaving it, now it was his for always. It was late, but sleep was far away. Robert didn't want it to come yet anyway, he wanted to lie awake and savour the delights of the day that had just passed, and of the many, many days to come, picking them over slowly, like rich fruit.

Through the rough archway in his room he could see Rachel's secret place. The rocking horse would be put back there, if they were able to buy it, Aunt Em had promised. The ashes in the urn had been buried among the ancient Parry graves that lay half-buried in stones and moss in the tiny churchyard at Groeyurgoch. From the ruined wall you could stand

177

and lift your eyes up to the distant hills. It was a quiet resting place.

Robert thought about the Morgans. In his typically odd and unpredictable way, Gareth's father was letting him go to the new school in September and he was dead pleased about it, because now he could stay with his cousins in the town. But Robert wanted the change in Morgan to be more than skin-deep. Everybody deserved to be happy tonight.

He tried to remember Gareth's photograph, a young smiling man with his wife and son at his side, and the baby in his arms. But the picture would not come. If only Reg Morgan could find another wife, somebody to make him happy again, someone who'd look after Gareth, and Gran in her old age, someone like his mum.

But it would not come. He had said goodbye, now, to that world of fairy-tale, where everything is all right in the end. There was a reasonable chance that Gareth would cheer up a bit if his father really kept his promise about changing schools, and letting him stay with his aunt in Llandewi, and it certainly sounded as if life was going to be better for the Parrys too, from now on.

But would Morgan really change? Would he be happier? He'd probably just carry on in the dreary farm-house, yelling at Gran, and she would die there in the end, unthanked, doing for him. If only it could be different for everyone.

Robert himself was deeply and completely happy. He snuggled down in bed and listened to the night noises. Downstairs his parents sat by the fire, listening to Aunt Em's old gramophone. They'd put on the record that Gareth had brought, for Mum. 'What is life to me without thee? What is left if thou art dead?' It was the lament of Orpheus for his lost Eurydice.

He closed his eyes, thinking of the dead singer, eternal in her music, of Daniel Parry and his Rachel, of their own new Rachel asleep in his mother's arms. It was spring again. He thought of the hills and the commons, of the great trees by the house, and of all the everlasting things that were his already.

Paula Fox
One-Eyed Cat £1.99

Ned was unable to resist firing the gun just once. He aimed at a
shadow, a grey flicker in the autumn moonlight. His dread was that
someone had seen him. Yet no one punished him and Ned's
appalling anxiety and guilt grew. Was he responsible for blinding the
cat?

This brilliantly perceptive and powerful novel, set in the States in the
1930s is by the American novelist Paula Fox – winner of not only
the Newbery and Hans Christian Andersen medals, but also the
American Book Award for Children's Literature.

'Sometimes a rare book comes along that adults and children can
appreciate with equal intensity ... These exceptional books can be
read at multiple levels of understanding; they extend fresh insights to
grown-ups, yet remain within the grasp of the younger ... reader.
Such a book is Paula Fox's latest novel, *One-Eyed Cat*.'
CHILDREN'S BOOKS

Stephen Bowkett
Spellbinder £1.75

'I'm scared of it, Tony. You don't know how far it can go'
'It's OK. I'm controlling it'
Tony lay in his usual place on the bank. A green glass marble rested
in the air, an inch above the ground.

Tony's interest in magic meant he had a few tricks up his sleeve. But
it was all an optical illusion – speed of the hand deceiving the eye.
Until one day he made a coin totally disappear. Not even Tony knew
what was happening then, and it made him shiver.
When the school fete needed a professional magician, Tony was
asked to ring one. As he dialled, his heart began to thump. Someone
picked up the phone, and before he could utter a word, the voice
said: 'Hello, Tony. I've waited for your call.'

What was happening was real magic.

Joyce Dunbar
Mundo and the Weather-Child £1.95

'I hate the garden! I hate the house! I want to go back home.'

Edmund feels a stranger in the rambling house he and his parents have moved to, but by the time winter arrives, he is utterly lost. Unable to hear, he is locked into a solitary world of silence.

But, slowly, he discovers another world in the wild garden. There he makes friends with the Weather-Child, who climbs and rides on the weather, swinging on all its changes.

It is the Weather-Child who frees him from isolation and leads him back into the real world.

Betsy Byars
The Not-Just-Anybody Family £1.99

Boy Breaks into City Jail

It made all the headlines when Vern broke *into* prison, but what would you do if your grandpa was in jail? The Blossoms had no doubts. Since they couldn't get Pap out, Maggie and Vern had to get in. A little unusual, perhaps, but as Maggie said, 'We Blossoms have never been just "anybody".'

This is the first adventure for the Blossoms – Pap, Vern, Maggie, Junior and Mud the dog. They're a family you won't forget.

Douglas Hill
Planet of the Warlord £1.50

Keill Randor, last legionary of the planet Moros and his alien
companion, Glr, finally end their search for the evil that threatens the
galaxy when they come face to face with the true horror of the
Galactic Warlord. But even their combined power may not be
enough to smash the Deathwing army and save the galaxy from
destruction ...

Galactic Warlord £2.25

He stands alone ... his planet, Moros, destroyed by unknown forces.
His one vow – to wreak terrible vengeance on the sinister enemy.
But Keill Randor, the Last Legionary, cannot conceive the evil force
he will unleash in his crusade against the Warlord and his murderous
army, the Deathwing.

Deathwing Over Veyna £2.25

The Robot's attack proved one thing – that the Deathwing was on
the Cluster with a weapon that could destroy a world.

Only a small rebellion in a minor solar system but it was part of the
evil master-plan of the mysterious Galactic Warlord. And it would
need all the special skills and courage of Keill Randor, the Last
Legionary, and his alien companion Glr, to defeat the Deathwing,
and save the planet Veyna.

All Pan books are available at your local bookshop or newsagent, or can be ordered direct from the publisher. Indicate the number of copies required and fill in the form below.

Send to: **CS Department, Pan Books Ltd., P.O. Box 40, Basingstoke, Hants. RG21 2YT.**

or phone: 0256 469551 (Ansaphone), quoting title, author and Credit Card number.

Please enclose a remittance* to the value of the cover price plus: 60p for the first book plus 30p per copy for each additional book ordered to a maximum charge of £2.40 to cover postage and packing.

*Payment may be made in sterling by UK personal cheque, postal order, sterling draft or international money order, made payable to Pan Books Ltd.

Alternatively by Barclaycard/Access:

Card No.   ☐☐☐☐☐☐☐☐☐☐☐☐☐☐☐☐

Signature:

Applicable only in the UK and Republic of Ireland.

While every effort is made to keep prices low, it is sometimes necessary to increase prices at short notice. Pan Books reserve the right to show on covers and charge new retail prices which may differ from those advertised in the text or elsewhere.

NAME AND ADDRESS IN BLOCK LETTERS PLEASE:

....

Name ————————————————————————

Address ——————————————————————

————————————————————————

————————————————————————

————————————————————————

3/87